LEMON

LEMON
A 304 Love Story

T. STYLES

BY T. STYLES

Are You On Our Email List?

Sign Up On Our Website

www.thecartelpublications.com

4

LEMON

WWW.THECARTELPUBLICATIONS.COM

BY T. STYLES

LEMON: A 304

LOVE STORY

BY

T. STYLES

PUBLISHER'S NOTE:
This book is a work of fiction. Names, characters, businesses,
Organizations, places, events and incidents are the product of the
Author's imagination or are used fictionally. Any resemblance of
Actual persons, living or dead, events, or locales are entirely coincidental.

Library of Congress Control Number: 2025913759

ISBN 10: 978194837X

ISBN 13: 9781948373999

Cover Design: Book Slut Girl

First Edition

Printed in the United States of America

8

BY T. STYLES

What up Fam,

Man, it's been a crazy time in my family since I last penned y'all a note. Right after we dropped, "A Weird Peace" in January 2025, my mom got sick and had to go to the hospital. She was diagnosed with an aggressive, Brain Glioma. Which translated means, a fast-growing brain tumor, and she had two of them. There was no cure for it and Chemo and Radiation could have possibly slowed it down but would not stop it. Wouldn't have mattered anyway because my mom refused treatment.

So needless to say, my world was flipped on its head and became a roller coaster of emotions for the next 4 months after. She passed away on Tuesday, May 20, 2025. Although, this whole situation seemed like it was on speed, my mom got what my wife called, "The Package". She was able to be visited by friends and family from all over the nation. She wasn't in pain, she got to eat what she wanted and got loved on up through the day she passed. God gave us all a gift as we had time to show and tell her how much we loved her. For this, I'm truly grateful! 🙏

It's been harder than I thought it would be dealing with my mommy being gone, but I'm working through it. If you're a praying person, please keep me and my family in your prayers.

In honor of the life of my mommy, I'm giving the love in this novel to:

SHEILA M. WASHINGTON
August 21, 1952 – May 20, 2025

Rest in eternal peace Lady, we love you and will miss you immensely!

Bye now! 💜

Aight Fam, thank y'all for listening. Now go'on and jump into this book. This story reminds me of *Classic* T. Styles. It's a heartfelt, edge of your seat tale that had me in a chokehold! Straight 🔥 so I know you gonna love it! 🖤

BY T. STYLES

As always, love & light!

C. Wash

Vice President

The Cartel Publications

www.thecartelpublications.com

www.facebook.com/authortstyles

www.facebook.com/Publishercwash

Instagram: Publishercwash

Instagram: Authortstyles

www.facebook.com/cartelpublications

www.theelitewritersacademy.com

Follow us on IG: Cartelpublications

Follow our Movies on IG: Cartelurbancinema

#CartelPublications

#UrbanFiction

#prayforcece

#ripmommy

#LEMON

BY T. STYLES

A lemon can be used for many things.
Cleaning, healing and eating. But I never realized
how many ways a body could be used until they
destroyed mine.

PROLOGUE

*S*he beat the rain but it didn't matter.

Because Lemon, who was tatted from head to toe, knew something was off before she even reached the front door. It wasn't the silence. The old brickhouse where she rented a room was usually quiet. It was a solid build that meant whatever you wanted to do behind one of its six-bedroom doors would remain a secret.

Nah, this was different.

As her long cream-colored legs moved toward the building, a sense of dread took over her soul. It worsened when she opened the door and was unpleasantly surprised.

It was the smell.

Warm, metallic, like burnt plastic and something sweet gone bad. A thick scent that stuck to the back of her throat forcing her to relive the odor every time she swallowed.

Her door, the one upstairs, toward the side hallway where her neighbor Victor loved to sneak women in while cheating on his wife, was cracked open. When she looked down, she saw a patch of red hair caught in the latch.

"What...what is this?" She frowned.

Her mind went on a tour as she looked at the strands trying to determine the owner. She didn't know anyone with

14

red hair. And when she pushed the door wider, more hair fell onto her damp doorway. Picking it up, she noticed it was clumped up.

Was it burned?

She was now sure the hair was synthetic which would account for the odor.

The next thing she felt was water sloshing at the heels of her shoes, seeping on the soles of her feet. Her cheap rug was dark and heavy with liquid, curling at the edges like it wanted to escape.

"Fuck is this?" After some research and a headache that would not let her go, she noticed the sink was on in her bedroom. Not just running...pouring. "Who...been in here?"

Wanting to understand while also being afraid, she stepped deeper inside, slow and careful.

The water had overflowed onto the counter. Her combs, the cheap bottle of edge control, the shea butter she rationed, and her makeup was all swimming in liquid.

But nothing was taken.

Just water pouring over everything she cherished plus the red clumpy hair.

And then she turned toward the bed.

And froze.

There, on the pillow, was more hair. Picking it up, she felt as if the floor had dropped from up under her.

Because she knew exactly what it meant now.

CHAPTER ONE

He was done with my mother, and now it was my turn.

She never could finish him off, which is why for as long as I can remember, when she moaned and went to sleep, he would come to me for a 'completion'. To say how much I hated this man, and what he was doing to me and my mother, would not do my words justice. So I stopped speaking...stopped complaining.

And prayed he would die.

It didn't work.

Here he comes...I saw his tall, fat silhouette.

From the bottom of the door, lighting up the floor in the hallway, his footsteps pressed into the wood as he moved toward me. I swear to God, I wish he would fall through into someone else's bed. And leave me alone.

But I never got my wish.

Instead, I took a deep breath and turned to my phone, "I gotta go," I told Smack, my boyfriend.

I felt his rage. "You know what, I'm sick of that nigga. How you expect me to feel 'bout this shit?"

"You talking to me as if I don't feel the same way. But there's nothing I can do right now."

"You been saying that shit for years. How about you take your red ass to the police."

"You know I can't do that."

I get why he felt the way he did, but telling Marco no wasn't an option. I had to do what he wanted, or he would cause problems for my mother and me. By doing stuff like not helping pay the rent. Turning off my cell phone. Buying groceries. Spiteful shit like that to make my mother work long drawn-out hours.

My mother had a job as a manager of a restaurant, but it barely paid anything. And since I wasn't employed, we needed him. I didn't want to see her cry like I had so many times before. So I would rather cry to myself. And pretend things were OK.

"He about to be in here and you know he pay for my cell phone so −."

"I'm not getting off the phone, Jay. Not this time. Fuck that nigga."

He's done this before, and it always weirded me out. Who would want to listen to something like this? "But he's gonna −."

"Just leave the phone open."

"But I don't want you to hate me for it. I don't want you to leave me."

"Do it!"

BY T. STYLES

Quickly I stuffed it into the cushion and before I knew it, my mother's boyfriend walked up to me. Smelling like her lotion and sweat. "Your momma got tired again. You ready for me?"

Without waiting on an answer, because it was never a question, he dropped his boxers over his round hips, and they fell around his ashy ankles.

Once on my side, I rolled on my back and tucked the phone even deeper within the cushion, hoping that my boyfriend wouldn't hear what was coming next. Without another word, he kissed me hard, his chapped lips scratching against mine.

He allowed the fullness of his body to press against me and I could hardly breathe.

Next he took his hands and pulled down on my hips as he entered me over and over. Since I was older now and knew what he wanted, to be exact, I learned what to do to make him cum quicker. To move my hips, to moan and to tell him it felt good.

All lies...but it always worked. And then it was over.

When he was done he got up without so much as a thank you. He used to tell me I was prettier and cleaner than my mother. Shit he felt I wanted to hear. But I was an adult, so he didn't offer me the lies anymore, figuring I knew the truth instead.

That both my mother and me belonged to him.

I wiped his creamy cum off of my belly with my own shirt and then tossed it on the floor. It would end up crusty white like the rest of my clothes when he got finished with me.

When he was gone, I cried so long that I forgot about Smack.

When I grabbed the phone, he had hung up.

My favorite thing to do was shower.

I would do everything inside the bathroom...sing, dance and even eat.

It was always better when I had the apartment to myself because I didn't have my own room. The only bedroom in the house went to my mother and Marco leaving me to sleep on the couch. But that's if they didn't have one of those parties that lasted all night, then I would have to stay over my best friend Mariah's.

BY T. STYLES

Right now, I had my phone on the sink...and the music loud. It was my magical place where I could forget about it all. As the water ran over my body, I lathered the washcloth as much as possible so I could wash away his smell.

I needed to feel new.

I was really getting into a *Muni Long* song when my phone rang. Hoping it was him, I almost slipped trying to grab it. Please let it be my boyfriend.

The moment I heard the voice I was disappointed. It wasn't Smack, it was my friend Mariah.

"Oh...it's just you." I wiped the soap out of my tatted-up face and crossed my arms, my butt pressing against the sink.

"Damn, bitch...fuck you say it like that for?"

"Sorry, girl. I was just expecting...you know what...what's up?"

"You coming over right?"

I didn't feel like going over her house. Whenever I went over it was always some stupid shit popping off. Either she was fighting Jordan, her boyfriend, or she was popping pills causing us to get into trouble. The worst times would be when she would throw up a few feet from where I would end up sleeping on the floor since she didn't have a sofa.

Things could be tragic when we were together, at the same time, she was the friend that if I ever needed to sleep over, she would give me a clean sheet and a soft pillow. She the kind of friend I hoped I could be, once I got my shit together.

Because right now I feel useless to everyone, even myself.

"Yeah, I'll be over later. I just gotta finish washing up first."

"You mean taking a long ass shower until them people's water run out?"

"Mariah, I—."

"Girl, if you tell that fat ass nigga to stop touching you, you wouldn't need—."

"Mariah, stop!" I yelled. "Please."

Silence filled up the space. She had a way of trying to help me that did more damage instead.

"I know you don't wanna hear it, but until you tell your mama what her man is doing to you, you'll never be clean. Like I said, I don't care how many showers you take. What...You don't think she'll believe you? Because—."

"I'll see you in a minute. I love you."

"I love you too," she sighed. "I just don't want both of us to be out here fucked up before we have kids. Cause we breaking the generational curse shit."

I don't know why she kept thinking our situations were the same. Me and my mother were close, like best friends. And Mariah didn't even know who her family was. She grew up in foster care all her life. So on everything I wish she stopped saying that shit.

Exhausted with her, I called my boyfriend instead. I knew Smack wasn't gonna answer but—"Hello."

I was shocked. He did answer.

Whenever he knew Marco was on top of me the night before, he would ignore my call for days. So for him to answer so quick was different. "What you doing?"

"What you want, Jay? I'm busy."

I wrapped myself in my red towel. "You still mad at me?"

"I'm mad I gotta share you with a rapist if that's what you mean. And as far as I'm concerned, your mother's in on it."

I felt my body heat up. He didn't know my mother and wasn't as close to her as I was. She would never allow him to touch me if she knew. I would bet my life on it.

"That's a lie! I never told her and if I did she would stop it."

"So you like it? What he paying you or something?"

"Smack, I can't—."

"You know what, it don't even matter. I'm sick of that nigga. If it's not him it's Giant. Who been circling around you ever since I can remember."

"I never even talked to Giant."

Giant was a pimp who whenever I would need a few dollars would give it to me. Unlike other girls he would make them work for their money, but for some reason he treated me different. And I never knew why. It don't matter because I haven't talked to him in over a year, even though I sometimes catch him watching me from across the street in his Benz.

"Don't mean the nigga not laying in wait. You gotta understand where I'm coming from. And at the end of the day, you gotta move out, Jay. You nineteen so what the fuck you waiting on? Because if you don't leave, and soon, you gonna lose me."

BY T. STYLES

I was walking out my apartment and into the hallway when I heard screaming. When I opened the door I saw Ava slapping her twelve-year-old daughter Hazel in the face.

What the fuck? She really out here hitting friend.

I dropped my purse and grabbed Ava's loose black hair, before giving her the same energy in the face. I'm talking about as hard as I could with an open hand. I was hitting her so hard her Latino and black features jiggled. I learned somewhere that fighting like this always threw people off, because most folks expected punches. But slaps kept your nails fresh and stunned your opponent.

"Get off me, bitch!"

But I didn't though. I wouldn't stop until I felt her slick blood under my fingertips, from my nails scratching her cheek. "Jaystar, please stop!" Hazel said. "You're hurting her!"

When I looked at her scared face, I saw my own and let her mother go. As much as I hated this woman and how she treated Hazel, I wouldn't want anyone to hurt my mother either.

"You gonna wish you never put your hands on me!" Ava yelled.

"Promises, promises," I said, wiping her blood back on her shirt. "You ain't have no business putting hands on this little girl."

"You know what, if you want her so bad, you keep her! Since she don't wanna listen to nobody."

"It's whatever!" I yelled grabbing Hazel's hand before smoothing her baby hairs back in position, that sat in front of the two long French braids that ran down her back. "Because wherever she goes right now will be better than this shit."

Ava wiped her hair out of her face and touched her bloody lips. "You sure about that?" She laughed. "And where she gonna sleep? On the couch with you?"

She's right.

I ain't have shit but whatever I had Hazel could have half. "Don't worry about it, bum bitch."

With that, me and Hazel walked out of the apartment door on the way to Mariah's which was a few buildings over. I always took the back route because I hated walking in the front even though the buildings were kinda close.

The more I walked the more I realized I might have fucked up. I guess talking to Mariah and Smack threw me off because what the fuck? How I look taking care of somebody and I was sleeping on a floor or couch.

26   BY T. STYLES

As we moved down the street, I was so mad I forgot why I was angry until I felt Hazel's arms wrap around my waist.

Back in my body, I looked down at her and rubbed her braids. She ain't need to say nothing. I got her. We in the same boat, just on different ends of the hallway.

CHAPTER TWO

We hadn't even been there thirty minutes before all hell had broken loose.

Let me backtrack a little...I love my friend. Mariah had that kind of beauty you couldn't bottle. Brown skin, skinny, long fingers that talked while she did, and big eyes that always looked like they were scheming.

Since she lived on the third floor of a building where the elevator worked only when it felt like it, the hallways always smelled like weed, bleach, or fried chicken, all depending on the day. Stank floated to the top first...everybody knew that. So when I walked up the steps I always felt like I had to throw up.

But there was something about her...even in the chaos that for me was a safe place.

"Hey, girl," Mariah said as I came through the door, wrapping her arms around me too tightly before I pushed her off.

She be doing too much sometimes.

When we separated and I laid eyes on her, I knew she'd already started her pill-popping process. That meant anything was possible.

"Ooh, and you brought Hazel," she added, reaching out and grabbing one of her braids. "How come you so pretty? You 'bout to be driving them little boys crazy."

Hazel shook her head, looking unimpressed. She had been around Mariah enough to know her moods too. In other words she knew the bitch was high. "You must be feeling good, huh?"

"Not as good as I wanna be," Mariah responded, eyes glassy. Then Mariah looked at me, like she was looking through me. "So since I can tell something wrong, what we drinking?"

I looked at Hazel and back at her. "I'ma chill tonight."

Her jaw dropped in the dramatic way it usually did when she wanted to be overboard. "Why the fuck you not drinking?"

"What you mean why? You sound crazy."

You'd think being my friend, she would've encouraged me to hold back. "I mean I'm not with all the sober shit. Not tonight anyway. We celebrating."

"Celebrating what?"

"I'm getting married."

"Married? To who?" I asked, already skeptical. "Jordan?"

"Jordan? Nah, I'm done with him."

She was just talking to him two weeks ago.

The fuck?

So who was she marrying?

We walked deeper into the apartment and sat on folding chairs. "Then who?"

"To Walker," she said with a grin. "You know, the dude from the liquor store that wanted your yellow ass first. Remember? We met him what...three weeks ago?"

I shook my head. "First of all he ain't want me. I was just the first person he saw."

"Don't worry about all that," she snapped. "Just know he 'bout to be my husband."

"Mariah, your pussy gonna fall out. I keep telling you."

"Ewww...," Hazel laughed.

"You gotta be careful, girl," I continued. "Don't be trusting niggas so easy. He look grimy."

"Listen, one day you gonna learn that you need a nigga for every occasion. Trust me, you'll see."

"Yeah, whatever."

Mariah liked to play these games all the time so there was no use in arguing. So I let it go. "It's like this," I said, dropping my bag on the floor. "Hazel might have to stay the night with me over here. If that's cool."

"Mmm," Mariah said, her tone suddenly softer. "With me? Ain't no problem. Wherever I am, you got a place too. And that goes for your surrogate daughter also." She grinned sinisterly. "But only *if* you drink with me."

"Pour me something white...not brown."

She hugged me like we hit the lottery as we walked off to the kitchen.

An hour later, the music was blasting, the bass shook empty bottles on the counter. Hazel was on the chair, eating a cheeseburger and fries with my cell phone in her lap scrolling. Every now and then I'd ask if I had any calls.

"Nope," she'd say, mouth full of meat.

I hope she ain't lying.

I needed my man to hit me back. But who knows at this point because he could hold a grudge. While Mariah was in the room I was watching her little dog nibble at the end of a frayed portable charger cord. Everybody knew them things were fire hazards and here she go letting him bite on it. I was just about to grab him when it happened.

A spark lit.

It flashed, loud and fast, and scared the hell out of me, Hazel and the dog too, who took off running across the living room with his tail tucked.

"Oh shit!" I yelled, jumping up. I grabbed a couple of jackets thrown over chairs around the kitchen table and tried to smother the flame. It wasn't working and I felt useless. Moments later Mariah came stumbling out the back room.

"What you do?!"

"What I do?" I snapped. "Your fucking dog was chewing on the portable charger, and it caught fire. So how you sound?"

"I'm sick of his ass," she said as we continued to try to put the fire out.

We scrambled, half-useless, swatting and smothering at the flames which were growing bigger. From the corner of my eye I saw that Hazel vanished for a second and came back with a bowl of water. Pushing between us, she tossed it, and finally the fire hissed out.

It took a child.

Embarrassing.

32   BY T. STYLES

The room stunk of charred plastic but at least we didn't burn this bitch down. With me in my head and Mariah high, we weren't worth much in an emergency. Thank God she was here.

I was still catching my breath when I sat down in one of the folding chairs. Just when I thought things couldn't get any worse it did. Because the front window exploded after a rock came flying through, shattering glass across the floor and into my locs.

"I know you fucking lying," Mariah said, charging out the front door like she'd been waiting for an excuse to be extra.

Of course I followed right behind her.

Once we got down the stairs and on the curb, there stood the biggest girl I'd seen in a long time. She was light skinned and her arms were crossed, and neck cocked to the side. The white shirt she had was sweaty and her jeans looked like she'd been rolling around in blood, dirt and paint. She was cracking her knuckles like she was warming up to fight. And all I wanted to know was how she throw that rock so far?

"Which one of y'all bitches fucking Walker?" She asked, eyes flicking between us.

I shook my head. I already knew Walker wasn't about shit and this proved my point. "Who you and what you doing here?" I asked.

"Is it you?" She said, stepping forward. "You fucking Walker?"

After the day and night I had, I decided I wanted all the smoke. "Yeah," I said. "It's me. Now what?"

Before I could say another word, she moved forward, and her fist connected with my face.

Hard.

But she had the right one because I was good. I loved to fight. I don't know why. But I was good at it. Part of me wished I didn't fight so much, to be honest. But something about it gave me peace...maybe a strange release.

So I knew even with the wine coolers I drank she still couldn't whoop my ass on my worst day. So I yanked her forward and pounded my fists into her face and temple.

Next thing I knew, Mariah jumped in, swinging like she was on fire. I guess it was too much because the girl backed up in an attempt to get away it seemed. The thing was, I wasn't done. I was thinking about losing Smack, about Marco and more. So I gave chase.

BY T. STYLES

But she must've been scared because she bolted for her car, peeling off just before I gripped her door handle and pulled her fat ass back to the concrete. While I was out of breath, angry she had gotten away too soon, Hazel stood on the porch behind us, laughing so hard she had to hold her stomach.

"Get in the house," I told her, shaking my head. "I can't believe you was back there watching anyway."

"Whatever you do, I'ma do too," she giggled. "You ain't see me kick her?"

I didn't.

"Girl, get in the building."

She went upstairs, laughing the entire way.

"You heard her right?" Mariah whispered. "She said everything you do she gonna do too."

"She just talking," I waved the air. "Anyway I knew that nigga wasn't shit."

"I know for a fact Walker not fucking that girl," Mariah huffed looking in the direction she drove.

"How you know?" I asked as we climbed the steps.

"Did you see her?"

"I did," I said. "But...pussy don't got no face."

We were sweeping up the glass from the broken window and trying to salvage what was left of the living room when Walker showed up. Six feet four inches tall and a bit wide, he came in talking too much, causing too many issues. Between the fire, the fight, and him acting a fool, there was no way me and Hazel were spending the night.

I didn't feel safe.

And didn't feel like pretending either.

So I packed up my stuff and grabbed Hazel's hand.

It was time to go home, a place I didn't want to be.

CHAPTER THREE

When we made it back to my building, sticky and sweaty, I climbed the steps with Hazel clinging tighter to my side. Like I said, my apartment door sat directly across from hers, and so I took a few moments to look down at her. Truth be told with Marco lurking, my house wasn't safe either.

But I wasn't going to make her do what she ain't wanna do.

"You ready to go home?" I asked gently. "Your mother may be sleep now. Maybe she won't bother you."

She didn't shake her head. Didn't open her mouth. But her eyes told me everything I needed to know.

She wasn't ready.

There was only one choice, she was staying with me.

I pulled my keys from my purse and unlocked the door. The living room was dark, and the couch, my bed, was free. That meant my mother and Marco were in their room. That gave me a little relief.

I didn't always see my mother at night, her energy mostly reserved for Marco. She worked during the day, and whatever strength she had left, she saved for him.

At first, it used to hurt my feelings.

But I wanted her happy and I know she wanted me to be too. Plus with Hazel here, I was just grateful that we had the couch to ourselves.

"Here," I said, handing her a towel, washcloth and soap. "You can use these to clean up."

She eyed the body wash I laid out and scrunched her nose. "Ew. This stuff gives me yeast infections."

I frowned. "What soap do you use?"

"Dove."

"I don't have Dove," I admitted. "But you can use the bar soap on the top shelf in the bathroom. The pink one. It's mine. Just try to be quiet, okay?"

She nodded, then surprised me by wrapping her arms around me, tight. It was almost like she didn't want to let me go. "Thank you, Jaystar."

I hugged her back, holding on longer than I expected. I felt her love, but I wanted to be honest too. She needed to know this wasn't permanent. I got a little money from my boyfriend, but he was already getting tired of me. Fifty dollars here, a hundred there, was barely enough to float by alone. But it definitely wasn't enough for me to care for someone else, even someone like Hazel.

While she showered, I fixed the couch to make it as comfortable as possible. My plan was to put her close to the cushions while I'd take the outer edge. That way, if *he* came, I could protect her.

I heard that plans are what fools make when they think they're in control. Whoever said that shit was right.

An hour later, we were both clean and lying on the couch.

The apartment was still.

As Hazel laid behind me, I heard her shift a little, the blanket rustling like soft paper.

"Are you okay?" I asked, not turning around just yet.

She took a breath deep enough to fill the room. "Does your mommy love you?"

The question hit harder than I expected. I held my voice steady, like I had to be sure...for her. "Yes," I said, pressing the words out with all the strength I had left in my heart. "Of course she does. We been through a lot, but it's always been her and me against the world."

I already knew where this was headed. She wanted to talk about her mother. And I'd been too afraid to go there, afraid of the hurt that might surface for both of us. But something about her voice tonight made me press it instead of running.

"Your mother loves you too, Hazel," I said gently, letting the silence carry the weight before I added, "It's just...the drugs got her mind that's' all."

"She hates me."

"It's impossible for mothers to hate their own."

Hazel nodded slowly behind me. I could feel her thinking. Then came another breath, heavier than the last. "I've never had a birthday cake," she said. "Never had a birthday party, either."

Silence.

Her voice stayed steady but soft. "The only thing I ever got was this Halloween costume from five years ago. I can't fit the outfit anymore, but I always kept the wig."

I rolled onto my back, halfway turning toward her.

"One day, I threw her drugs away," she went on. "I just wanted her to be okay. Because whenever she used, she'd let people in. People who hurt her. Sometimes me too."

My stomach knotted. But she kept talking.

"I didn't care too much about what they did to me. I just hated seeing her get hurt. That's the part I couldn't stand."

And in that moment, I knew. There was something inside Hazel, something raw and real and cracked in a way that matched the same fractures inside me. For the first time I believed in kindred spirits.

"Anyway," she continued, "when she found out, she got mad. Real mad. She burned the wig. Set it on fire and threw it in the sink. I guess to stop it from catching the rest of the house and burning it down. I was able to save a little of it until she found it and threw that away too."

"I'm sorry about that, Hazel."

"I didn't really care about the wig. Not the hair, anyway. What hurt was…for a moment, I started hating her. And I don't wanna hate her. You understand?"

Twelve years old.

She was only twelve years old.

I turned the rest of the way toward her and kissed her forehead. "Get some sleep," I whispered. "For now…you're safe."

Then I heard the same sound I always did...muffled satisfaction from down the hall. My mother, doing what she always did, giving what she always gave, leaving him wanting more.

This time I closed my eyes.

Please God, not tonight. Don't let him come, because the last thing I wanted was Hazel to see a real-life monster.

But prayers only work for everybody else but me.

When I opened my eyes, I saw his silhouette stretch across the floor first, outlined by the hallway light behind him. Then I heard his footsteps, deliberate, cruel, drawing closer.

He stopped in front of us.

"Oh, you got a friend tonight?" He said before licking his lips and gripping himself. "Hi, Hazel." He reached over me and grabbed her braid. "Your mouth is as pretty as your mama's. I wonder if it's just as wet."

I slapped his hand. "Leave her alone," I snapped, before she could even speak.

I didn't want her giving him anything, not even a smile. He didn't deserve her attention.

He laughed and raised two hands in the air before dropping them at his sides. "You ready for me then?"

He asked, voice lower. She can sleep on the floor but I'm getting what I came for. So what you —."

"No."

"Bitch, is you crazy?" He said with a smirk, "you better get ready."

Before he could touch either of us again, I jumped up and lashed out. I'm talking about slaps to his face, his chest, his stomach. Wild. Angry. I didn't know where the energy came from, only that it was time for me to defend myself.

To defend us.

Before long I felt his low energy body weaken under the hits, and finally, he backed off. "You're gonna wish you hadn't done that," he whispered, stumbling away.

Hazel wrapped her arms around me from behind. "Is he gone yet?" She whispered while trembling.

"Yes...I'm so sorry about that shit, Hazel."

"It's okay."

"Get some sleep," I said, rubbing her hand that squoze my belly. "We'll be fine. At least tonight."

The next morning, I got her ready for school with some of my clothes. They hung off her a little, but she didn't complain. When she was dressed I said, "I'll be outside when your bus drops you off out front. We'll come up with a plan then."

"I really appreciate this," she said.

"I don't know how long it can last, with you living here, but I'll do what I can. That's all I can promise," I said softly.

"You're my best friend."

And in that moment, after yesterday's conversation, I realized she was mine too.

After Hazel left for school, I walked to the kitchen. My mother was there, hair tied in a loose bun, wearing a t-shirt and gray sweatpants. She moved around the fridge like it was any other day.

I stared for a long time, just watching her. My mother was the prettiest woman in the world. She was a shade browner than me with naturally red cheeks and freckles. People would mistake us for sisters and she

BY T. STYLES

and I both loved it. When she was happy something smiled inside of me. I just love her that much.

But now it was time to get serious.

"Mommy..."

She turned, smiling as she pulled me into a hug and playfully tugged two of my lemon-colored locs.

"Hey, pretty girl," she said, before returning to her task.

"I have to talk to you about something."

"Okay. What's it about?"

My hands trembled.

My chest ached.

"It's about...Marco."

Her body went still. Not a muscle moved. She really looked like a statue. A beautiful one at that. "I don't wanna talk about him right now," she said sharply.

I stared. "What you mean you don't wanna talk about him? You don't even know what I'm gonna say."

"I said what I said. I don't want to talk about him."

"Mommy, it's just—"

"Listen," she cut in. "We'll talk about him later. Right now, I need to clean out this refrigerator because I'm going grocery shopping, and that's my only focus. So instead of wasting time, either help me or shut up."

"Mommy, I—."

"You want anything or not, Jaystar?" She yelled. "Because it's obvious you aren't listening to what the fuck I'm saying!"

I opened and closed my mouth several times, before tugging one of my locs. "Strawberry yogurt. And Captain Crunch cereal."

She nodded. "I'll grab it when I go shopping."

"Thank you. I didn't mean to make you upset. I just—."

"And since we talking, at some point, Jaystar, you need to find a job. It can't just be me and Marco taking care of everything around here anymore. You a woman now."

That part stung more than anything, because I sure didn't feel like one.

Later that day, I was sitting in McDonald's with my boyfriend, eating cold fries and a cheeseburger I wasn't really hungry for. I was happy when he decided to take me to get something to eat, but my appetite was done.

"How you doin' over there?"

BY T. STYLES

I loved when he asked me that. Not because I couldn't handle things. But because it meant...maybe...he still cared.

"I'm fine," I said. "I really am. I just...I don't wanna lose you."

He leaned back, smirking. "Well, if you don't wanna lose me, you know what that means."

"What you expect me to do?" I asked. "I don't have a job. Me and my mother—"

"It's just you," he interrupted. "And I wish you'd stop pretending otherwise. The only person you should look after is yourself."

I didn't respond.

Just pulled the soda bottle from my purse and twisted the cap.

It wasn't soda by the way.

I took a long drink, the warm vodka slipping down my throat, burning and numbing at the same time. It made me feel light. Like I could still laugh, even if everything was falling apart.

"You wanna go to the car?" I asked. "So I can put a smile on your face. Suck your dick and swallow the way you like?"

"Nah, I'm good on that."

I wanted to crawl up under the building.

"You know what I really want. And until you give me that, there's not much to talk about."

Then he took my fries and walked out.

I was sitting in my old but faithful car, a silver Altima, and checked my watch. Hazel would be out of school soon. With the night she had I wanted to make sure she was okay. I wanted her to know that I was still here, even though I didn't have a plan.

I got out and rushed to the bus stop. A few minutes later, the kids began to pour off the bus. From afar, I could see Hazel scanning the street, searching.

Then she saw me.

She smiled like I was the sun rising just for her.

Think about that...worthless, broken me, able to make someone like her feel seen. Maybe things aren't as bad as I once thought.

She told me about her friends Shawny, Leslie and Keisha as we walked down the street. How Shawny talk too much and how Leslie is so sweet. I nodded but to be honest they sounded a little faster than I liked.

Suddenly both of us got quiet when we reached our apartment building. Once inside I glanced at her door…then mine. We wouldn't even bother about going to her house because her eyes told me all that needed to be told.

Instead, I stuck the key in the lock to my apartment.

It wouldn't turn.

I tried again. Still nothing.

"Is everything okay?" Hazel asked, eyes wide.

"Yeah," I lied. "Everything's fine."

But then I smiled.

Because I hoped…maybe, just maybe, my mother put him out. That she listened even though I didn't get out what I wanted to say to her in the kitchen. Maybe words weren't needed and she believed me.

To confirm, I called her, over and over.

LEMON   49

But she didn't answer.

We waited at Mariah's place.

She was frying chicken, high as usual. Hazel ate like she hadn't eaten in days, but I couldn't stomach a thing.

"Girl," Mariah said, lighting another cigarette, "your mother locked you the fuck out. It's simple."

"No, I think she—."

"She didn't lock out Marco so hush with all that dumb shit. So you can either sit over there and look stupid or we can start brainstorming to figure out what you gonna do next."

"You don't know what you talking about."

"You can keep believing that if you want to, but the sooner you realize your mom's in on what's been happening to you…"

"Stop," I said. "You gonna make me not want to come back over here. And cut your ass off if you keep talking about my mother."

"Yeah, okay," she laughed. "If you go somewhere, I'm going too. We locked in for life. Which is why I'm

BY T. STYLES

gonna always tell you the truth. Whether you want to hear it or not because that's how much I love you."

As annoying as she was, that part made me smile.

Two hours passed.

Still no call from my mother.

I went back to the apartment to see if I could get inside because trust me when I say this had to be a mistake. He was probably stressing her out which is why she hadn't told me yet that she put him out. It probably hurt too bad.

Hazel stayed behind at Mariah's.

When I made it to my building, I saw my mom's car was outside. Again I tried to get in, even knocked, but she didn't open the door.

The thing was, I heard their voices. As clear as if they were in the kitchen.

As I walked down the street, I wrecked my brain. What could all of this be about? I hadn't done anything wrong.

I didn't deserve this.

This shit hurt more than surgery with no anesthesia.

Back at Mariah's I was pissed the fuck off when I saw that Hazel was gone.

"Where's Hazel?" I asked closing the door behind myself.

"I sent her home," Mariah said. "Walked her over myself to be sure she got inside."

"No you didn't! I would've seen you."

"Nope. Not if you used the back like you always do. I prefer the front."

"So you dodged me on purpose because you knew I would be mad."

"Girl, hush."

I stepped closer. "You shouldn't've done that shit! You don't know what's going on! What her mother did to her!"

"I talked to her mom. She's at home. She's safe."

I stood there, stunned.

She took a deep breath, her voice lower. "Since your mother put you out, which she did, whether you wanna hear it or not, you're gonna be living with me for a while," she continued. "That means you need to earn money. And face the truth. Your mother chose him over you so the last thing you need is a twelve-year-old seeing all this shit."

She held out a plate.

My heart broke. I needed to be sure my little friend was okay. I took the plate and slapped it on the table. "I don't have no fucking skills that'll pay me, Mariah! That's what I'm trying to say!" I was in between a breathing attack and trying to cry at the same time. "You not fucking listening!"

"What about the nigga Giant? He been trying to put you on forever."

"Yeah but he might want me to put out for money!"

"Don't they all?" She threw her hands up. "Anyway, eat that chicken! Cause you gonna need your strength for what's about to happen next."

CHAPTER FOUR

I was on the floor again.

Mariah's living room carpet smelled like old hair grease and weed, and the pillow under my head was barely thicker than a folded towel. I used one of the throw blankets from back in the day when she had a couch, but it didn't reach past my knees.

I was uncomfortable, but I didn't care.

I wasn't trying to be comfortable. I was just trying not to think too hard.

My phone buzzed once. I grabbed it fast.

It wasn't mommy. Just a notification that pizza was on sale. Still, I stared at the screen for a second before flipping it over, face down. Where was my mommy?

I'd already called six times. Texted her things like *"Please call me,"* and *"Just let me know you're okay."* Left voicemails I didn't even want to hear myself repeat.

Nothing.

No response.

It looked like Mariah was right after all.

She had never ignored me like this before. Not even when she was mad.

I tried to tell myself her battery was probably dead. Or maybe Marco had taken her phone again or interrupted her service like he had done mine when I didn't satisfy him. Maybe she was somewhere loud, didn't hear it ring.

But under that soft, sweet version of the truth was Mariah's voice. "Your mama chose him over you. Fuck that bitch."

I closed my eyes hard.

No. That couldn't be real.

My mama would never. Not after everything.

We were close. Closer than most.

I still remember the night when I was eight years old, and she screamed louder than I'd ever heard. My daddy, Frederick, had raised his hand to hit her and something in me snapped. I ran at him, fists flying, all teeth and tears. I don't even think I hurt him, but I distracted him long enough for her to get away.

He was locked up later that week for burning a man to death in his car.

After that, it had always been us against it all.

Then Marco came. He was thinner then and somewhat cute. A construction worker with a thick Mexican accent I could barely understand. With time his English got better, and he got hornier. That's when he moved us into his apartment, where we stayed now. I didn't have a room, and he swore he would make me a section in the corner, with a bed, hidden from his gaze.

He never did.

Instead, he would visit me in the middle of the night. Tell me how pretty I was while the covers rustled with his thick hand. When she needed a break, I would do things to distract him from hurting her. Including being what he called a co-girlfriend to a man I hated since I was ten years old.

She told me I saved her the night my father almost killed her.

I believed her.

So why won't she save me now?

Mariah and Walker were arguing again, loud enough that I could feel the vibration through the floorboards. He was accusing her of cheating, she was calling him broke and sorry, and it was all so familiar it made my stomachache.

I turned over, pulling the blanket higher, curling my knees to my chest.

The apartment was dark except for the glow of the stove clock and the occasional flicker of headlights through the blinds.

I didn't want to cry, so I focused on breathing.

Slow.

Steady.

Still no call.

Still no text.

I tried to remember the last good moment I had with my mama. Maybe it was when I did her hair in the kitchen, both of us sipping cheap wine and talking about a new start. She said Marco was going to leave soon. That she was tired. That we'd finally get back to the way things used to be.

Maybe that was the last lie she told me with love in her eyes.

Just then a door slammed down the hall. I flinched, but I didn't move.

Eventually, the yelling turned to sexual groaning.

Then loud moans followed by silence. Since he wasn't coming for me, only then could I sleep.

CHAPTER FIVE

The rain hit the car windows in waves.

I sat in the backseat of the Uber, phone clutched in both hands, thumb hovering over the call button like it would work better if I prayed harder. I decided to take a ride instead of using my car, hoping to be incognito.

I'd already tried my mother four times on the ride over.

Nothing.

Voicemail. Straight through.

Again.

The thought that she didn't love me anymore made my stomach twist as I pressed my forehead to the window and watched the city blur past streetlights.

I didn't realize we were close to the destination until the driver slowed down in front of Smack's house.

His car was in the driveway.

Wait a minute...so was he.

With her.

Was I seeing the girl he told me he broke up with to be with me? The one who fucked his cousin and best friend to get back at him.

Yep, it was her.

BY T. STYLES

I blinked through the rain, even leaned forward to get a better look.

They were in the front seat, her hands on his face, his mouth on hers. Kissing like they had all the time in the world. Like I didn't exist. So I called him again…and I know my call went through because the light from his screen lit up his chin.

He was ignoring me.

My throat closed. I could barely breathe.

"You getting out?"

"Yes…but…please wait," I told the driver, voice sharp. "I'll pay you I just…just wait here."

I climbed out into the storm, the cold water slapping against my legs as I ran up to the car. My shoes were no help as I slipped in the mud and my shirt clung to my body.

I knocked on the window hard, harder than I should have.

Smack looked up.

And blinked like I was a stranger.

He didn't even look surprised.

He rolled the window down halfway, eyes dull. "Can I help you?"

Can you help me? Fuck was this nigga on.

The girl looked at me too...real pretty, glowing, like she hadn't cracked me in half.

"Are you serious right now?" I asked, rain streaming down my face like tears I didn't give permission to fall.

He shrugged. "I don't know what you want me to say."

"Let's start with your first lie, do you know me or not?

He looked past me.

Like I was nothing.

Like I wasn't just texting him an hour ago, telling him I needed him. Like I hadn't curled up beside him last week, breathing slow, feeling like maybe this time someone would choose me back.

The girl smirked. "Edward, who is this bitch?"

Not his government name.

"Whoever you are, now is not the right time," he told me.

I backed away before I did something I couldn't take back.

Ashamed, I turned and walked back to the Uber, each step heavier than the last. By the time I closed the door behind me, I couldn't feel my feet anymore.

BY T. STYLES

"Back home?" The driver asked, glancing at me through the rearview mirror.

I opened my mouth.

But nothing came out.

My hands were shaking. My head was spinning. I stared at the water collecting on the inside of the window.

And then it hit me.

I didn't even know where home was.

CHAPTER SIX

Marco turned off my phone and I had to get another. Instead of getting one just for myself I got one for Hazel too with the last money that Smack had given me. Four hundred and eighty-three dollars I saved, and I was glad I wasn't a glamour girl who needed more than a little. I'm just a hood bitch who liked cropped tops, ripped shorts, jeans and coconut scented locs.

I had my heart broke already, so I might as well get it broken again.

So there I was, standing outside the diner in Pikesville, holding a bouquet of yellow roses, her favorite. The kind with the softest edges and scent she liked. I'd wrapped them in brown paper, just like the ones she used to get from Mr. Johnny down the block when she still smiled on Sundays.

He was older but I wish she stayed with him.

He never saw me as anything other than a little girl.

When I entered the bell chimed softly when I pushed the door open. The air inside was warm, greasy, and full of the smell of coffee, bacon fat, and maple syrup.

She was sitting at one of the corner tables, arms folded, eyes scanning a clipboard. Her lips moved just

BY T. STYLES

slightly, speaking something to herself, probably checking off another task.

When our eyes met, she paused.

Just for a second.

Did I see hate?

She started to stand, and I moved closer.

"Whatever this is about, just know that I have to get back to work," she said.

Whatever this is about? Why was I being tossed away all week?

Before I could speak, a younger waitress, barely older than me, appeared beside her. "You got twenty more minutes," the girl said, voice chirpy. "Just reminding you like you asked."

Like you asked?

Did she tell her to remind her just in case they saw me?

Either way I got the message. We didn't have a lot of time. She just motioned to the empty seat across from her. "Sit."

I did.

Quietly.

My hands trembled as I placed the flowers on the table, but she didn't reach for them. So I got up, and set them down beside her instead, on the bench. With them carefully in position, I took my seat again. One of the petals loosened itself and fluttered to the floor like it didn't belong.

It didn't get a chance to just be, before her heel landed on it as she shifted in her seat.

Maybe she didn't notice.

But I did.

"Why'd you change the locks?" I asked, voice barely steady.

She didn't look at me. "It's time for you to grow up. Make it on your own."

I blinked.

Swallowed.

"You couldn't have a conversation with me first, mommy?"

"I'm telling you now."

Why was she being so mean? "I don't have anywhere to go."

"You have your father's people," she replied, still avoiding my eyes. "You should try them."

"I did," I lied. Outside of my cousin Sheree, I didn't fuck with any of them. They were too jealous. "You know they not gonna help me though. They don't even like me."

She didn't respond. Just adjusted her watch like the seconds on it mattered more than my words.

"Please," I whispered. "Can you just...reconsider? Can I come back?"

Still nothing.

She stood up.

Scooped the flowers off the bench like they were something she was forced to carry. No glance. No thank you.

And then she walked away.

Just like that.

I watched her disappear through the swinging kitchen door. And just before it closed behind her, I saw it—

The bouquet hitting the top of the trash bin before dropping inside.

CHAPTER SEVEN

The sky was still the color of steel. Like it hadn't made up its mind if it wanted to rain. I hadn't seen Hazel in days and needed to check on her. After parking I walked fast, not because I was late, but because I had this feeling in my gut I couldn't shake. Like something was about to happen.

Or already had.

When I turned the corner, I saw her.

Hazel.

Sitting on the steps of our building with her little pink and black backpack hugged to her chest. She didn't see me at first. She was staring straight ahead, quiet. Still. Like something inside her had stopped moving. She also had her friends Leslie, Keisha and Shawny with her. They stood in front of her talking. But it was as if they were talking to themselves. I know that look. When you with people but checked out...mind on the worst of it all.

And then I saw it.

The bruise.

Right side of her cheekbone. Not fresh, but not old either.

BY T. STYLES

She turned and finally noticed me.

She didn't say anything.

She didn't need to.

I was fucking LIVID!

Her friends hugged her and walked off as I made my way to her. I just took her hand and said, "You not going back to your house. I don't give a fuck."

Her fingers curled tighter around mine, and I saw her smile.

Wide.

So full of trust it broke me open because I used to be this way with my mother.

"Where we going?" She asked.

I looked out toward the street, cars hissing past with wet tires and muffled music. "I don't know." Then turned back to her. "And I hope you don't mind that. Because...because I'm fucked up. But I care about you and will do all I can to keep you safe."

Hazel didn't answer with words.

She wrapped her arms around my waist, burying her face against my chest like I was something safe.

And in that moment, I knew....

Whatever came next, I wasn't alone.

CHAPTER EIGHT

My cousin Sheree owned an entire boarding house that leaned like it had secrets. The steps creaked loud enough to wake a whole block, and the railing wobbled every time you grabbed it, like it didn't want to be held.

Still, it felt better than where I'd come from.

Mariah's house.

After knocking when she opened the door, I didn't even say hello. I just stood there, eyes heavy, shoulders heavier. She was a shorty with a short blonde haircut and a bullet wound on her shoulder and thigh. Despite it all, her body was banging, and she couldn't hide it even if she tried.

"I need a place to stay."

Sheree sighed.

She didn't look surprised.

"So it's true. She put you out?"

Silence.

"You know staying here ain't free," she said, stepping aside so I could come in.

Her house was big, clean, lived in, and safe. I could deal with old.

"I know...I need to rent one of your rooms. But I ain't coming alone."

She looked me up and down, then her eyes drifted past me to Hazel, who was standing on the bottom step, fidgeting with the straps of her backpack.

"Y'all gonna stay in one room?"

"I won't move in here unless she's coming with me."

She shook her head. "I can't believe you're helping her when you can hardly help yourself."

I turned to look at Hazel and then back at Sheree. Before I could even open my mouth to answer, a truck pulled up to the curb outside. The engine rumbled deep and smooth.

I knew who it was.

I didn't even have to look.

It was him.

Giant.

He pulled up like he had perfect timing, like he was used to making entrances that couldn't be ignored. And just like before, my stomach flipped, then twisted, then dropped. He rolled the window down, flashing that smile that made women want to sell themselves just to be around him.

I knew the effect he had and watched him close as Sheree stepped out with me, arms crossed.

He leaned out the window, that gold chain catching the light just enough. "You ready?" He asked me.

I nodded and looked at my cousin. I've seen hate on a person's face before. Once when Old Lady Beverly hit Stone's motorcycle from behind, causing it to be totaled. He tossed the woman down and everything before he was curb stomped by everybody in my building for his efforts. And the other time was when I walked into my mother's restaurant with flowers.

But I never saw hate as heavy as how my cousin looked at Giant. There was history I just didn't know what.

"That's who you banking on? A nigga that throw fight parties just to sell bitches."

"He's how I'm gonna pay you," I said, voice quiet. "So me and Hazel can be good."

Sheree shook her head. "This ain't the way. He's trouble, cuz. I swear on everything I love."

"Well I'ma entertain him...even if just for a little while."

CHAPTER NINE

Later on that day, once Hazel was settled into the room I called Giant back. It was time for me to put my shit to work.

He helped girls get money with tricking and at first I wanted to avoid him. But I had another person depending on me, so I had no choice.

When he called back and told me to come outside, I grabbed my purse and looked over at Hazel. "Stay in the room and don't leave. I got an order of pizza coming in thirty minutes."

"You sure you coming back?"

I walked closer. "I'm not your mother. I won't leave you. Trust me."

She smiled and I walked out.

The air was cool and sweet, like the world had been waiting on me. There he was leaning against his car, a big-bodied Benz, arms folded, watching me like I was the only person on the street. I was halfway to him when he walked up, grabbed my hand with a touch that made my heart stutter.

Once inside, sitting neatly on the seat, were a bouquet of flowers and a box of candy.

My breath caught.

Was this for me?

I slid into the passenger's seat, calm and composed. Then he reached back and handed me the flowers. "Thank you," I said, trying not to sound too hungry for more attention.

What was all this about? I was willing to work with him.

I didn't ask. Just inhaled and exhaled.

I wanted to know where we were going, but something about him, his calm, his confidence, told me not to. This wasn't the kind of man who wanted you to make or ask a bunch of questions.

He wanted you to ride and experience his rescue.

So I did.

Before long we ended up at a park. Not dinner. Not a movie. Just a quiet park with a rusted bench and the smell of honeysuckle in the air. If he wanted it like this, why the roses?

I didn't complain, though I had been hoping for something more. Maybe dinner. Lobster. Shit, I never had that. But I wasn't trying to act like a beggar. He got out, walked around, and opened my door again.

BY T. STYLES

Once outside, we sat down together. The bench creaked beneath us, birds chirped somewhere above, and the sky looked like it was melting into gold.

Then he turned to me, his voice gentle but direct. "So...tell me 'bout yourself."

He wanted to talk about me? But I was nothing.

It threw me off. "I don't think there's much to tell which is why I hit you." I said, unsure. "I want to change that."

He smiled. "Not much to tell? How you sound. You living, right?"

"I am."

"You breathing too, right?"

I didn't want to tell him no. Truth was, since he picked me up, it felt like I hadn't gotten a full breath. "I guess," I nodded.

He leaned back, looking at the sky. "So as long as you're living and breathing, there's always something to tell. So let me hear it."

I paused. Then gave him the basics. "I was in college. But when my mother needed my tuition for bills, I dropped out and gave her everything I had. I just ran out of that money about a month ago. Now I owe the government."

He nodded. "What were you taking up?"

"Business Administration."

He chuckled, almost like it didn't matter. "A throwaway course."

It stung. I actually liked business. Had dreams of running something one day...being my own boss. But I let it go.

"Tell me more," he said. "You got a man?"

My throat tightened. I thought about Smack. About everything I never wanted to speak out loud. "Not anymore."

He looked at me for a beat, then smirked. "So what you need from me?"

"For you to help me make money."

"What if I don't want to?"

My heart twisted with something I couldn't name. At the same time, I had a little friend who depended on me, so I needed to be tough. "Listen, I need to get out of my cousin's house and get a place of my own. If you can't help then—."

"Like I said, what if I don't want to? What if I want to make you mine?"

"What does that mean?"

"It means that I'll take care of you. Make sure you good."

"For free?"

74   BY T. STYLES

"Nothing is free. Anyway, I'm tired of talking." He sighed. "Let's sit in the back seat."

Before I knew it I had his dick in my mouth.

I was surprised at how clean he tasted.

I must have been doing an okay job because he kept nodding a lot, like, mm-hmm. Good girl. Good girl. Like he was gonna grade me from a paper.

His upper body was pressed against the window while I sat between his legs. He wanted to do many things in the car and luckily there was space. His finger went in and out of my pussy while I continued to suck, and I was getting wet in a way I never got before. Definitely not with Marco or Smack.

Right before he came, he looked me in my eyes, "I need you to swallow. So we can forever be connected."

I did.

When he bust he picked me up and kissed me. It tasted like water, and I wanted to kiss him for hours, but instead he opened my legs and slipped into me, and I felt like I was flying.

Would selling my body be like this?

I would soon learn the answer was *fuck no*.

Within seconds, I could see why they called him Giant. It was big, almost too big, but still managed its way inside me. He looked me in my eyes when I tried to look away but staring at him felt wrong.

Like I was breaking the law or something. Instead, he grabbed both of my ass cheeks and pushed in and out. This was a sensation that I can honestly say I never felt before.

A sensation of pressure, but also of pleasure.

"I need you to be willing to do anything for me." He said.

I nodded rapidly because I began to feel something different. It was a cross between peeing on myself and tingling.

Please don't let me pee on myself. "I'll do anything for you."

"You saying that now, but at some point you're going to have to prove it. Because 304 girls are pleasers."

"What's a 304 girl?"

"You."

I didn't know that within a matter of days that 3 0 4 would become my life, and I would get all the answers I needed.

But who cared in that moment. I experienced my first orgasm.

CHAPTER TEN

*T*he house was a monster and a party was under way.

One of the many parties Giant was known for.

Tucked into the tree-lined backroads of Baltimore County, the mansion stood wide and arrogant beneath a moonlit sky. It was the kind of house Lemon had only ever seen from a screen. White stone walls, arching windows glowing with gold light, and black luxury vehicles curled around the circular driveway like sleeping panthers.

Lemon stepped out of Giant's truck, her heels hitting the brick with a muted click. The air smelled like cigars, grilled meat, and spilled liquor. It was electric. People were everywhere. On the steps, the porch, the lawn, the sidewalks. Mostly men. Tall, drunk, rowdy. Their laughter broke through the bass pumping from inside, their shirts untucked, mouths stained with brown liquor.

And they noticed her.

Eyes followed Lemon like she was the only woman in the world as Giant kept her close. Some called out, others just stared, bold and unapologetic.

"Damn, who that?"

"She with Giant?"

"I got something she can hold."

A few even stepped toward her, licking their lips like they could taste her already. But Giant, tall, clean-cut, and sharp, gleaming with white gold chains, moved in front of her. "Not right now," he said to no one in particular, voice low but heavy.

The men respected it. They moved on, looking for more available prey. And Lemon, though she would never say it out loud, felt something tighten in her chest.

Protection.

Power.

He didn't hold her hand, but he placed it on her lower back, just enough to guide her, just enough to claim her and together they moved through the crowd.

Inside was another world.

It was rich, loud and chaotic.

The walls gleamed with warm light reflecting off crystal glasses and designer watches. Flat-screen TVs lined the walls, each one showing a different fight. One was MMA, another a pay-per-view boxing match.

Women with glossy lips and perfect curves walked through in tight dresses that barely held their bodies. Some were laughing with the men. Some were whispering deals. All of them were working.

Lemon didn't feel like one of them.

Not tonight anyway.

78   **BY T. STYLES**

Tonight, she was with Giant.

At his side.

His woman.

She wouldn't know it, but she was put on display.

And before long she would go to the highest bidder.

CHAPTER ELEVEN

Hazel was asleep next to me, her little arm draped across my waist like she trusted me more than she should. Her breath was soft and steady, the kind that only came from real sleep.

I stayed still, careful not to wake her.

The mattress dipped under us both, just barely wide enough to count as a bed. The blanket we shared was thin, but she didn't complain.

She never complained.

My phone screen lit up the room in a pale blue glow. I scrolled slow, almost guilty, reading article after article. Tabs open on things I told myself I wasn't really looking for.

How to get started ho'ing.

Tips for high-end clients.

How not to get killed as a 304.

Each click felt like a whisper in the dark.

I didn't know what I was expecting. Maybe a guide on how to make it all feel less dirty. Less desperate. Something that would tell me it was okay if I didn't have another option. That survival had fine print.

But no matter how many links I opened; they all said the same thing.

You don't do this unless you're out of choices.

I locked the phone and let it fall to the mattress beside me. My fingers brushed Hazel's hair, and I froze, afraid I'd wake her.

She didn't stir.

Just sighed, deep and peaceful.

I looked down at this girl who wasn't mine but had started looking at me like I was all she had. And maybe I was. Mariah told me she saw her mother naked from the waist down off Liberty Road in Baltimore. And that she was going down so bad, she couldn't give that diseased pussy away. But she didn't have to tell me what I already knew.

Ava was somewhere off in another high, slipping further away from life and her only child.

I didn't mean to become her mother.

But it was happening anyway.

And now, lying in this bed, with the only warmth between us coming from each other, I wondered—

Was I already failing her?

Because how do you tell a child not to follow your footsteps, when your own are leading you off a cliff?

I closed my eyes.

And let the questions crawl into the space between us.

"Jay..." Hazel said with her eyes closed.

Dang, she wasn't sleep. "Yeah."

"Promise me you won't leave me like my mama."

She made me say this at least once a day. I knew the weight of this statement. I wanted safety and love like this too, but who was I to play with her heart? And soul.

"I promise I'ma do the best I can by you. And if I can't I promise I'ma be real with you no matter what."

I guess she was comforted because she went back to sleep.

It became easy to understand after a few weeks that Giant wanted to be my boyfriend/pimp. He said he didn't see me hoeing for long and once I stopped he wanted us to get serious about each other.

I wanted to believe him, but it was hard.

Right now all I wanted was to drink, save paper and get me and Hazel a bigger place of our own. I was also saving up in case my mother needed help because I know she didn't want to be with Marco.

I was sure of it.

Despite her rejection of me.

One Saturday Giant came over and sat on the edge of the bed. Hazel was playing with a phone I bought her and he looked over at her from the doorway. He was wearing shades, but I could still see the reflection of his eyes. "How come you so pretty?" He asked.

She shrugged and blushed. "I 'on't know."

"Well you are," he continued. "You gonna break some man's heart."

Something felt off. I didn't like his energy. So I decided to make my opinion known. "She's a kid, Giant," I told him.

"I know." He looked at her again and then back at me. "So let's talk about—."

"I don't want to talk about it in here." I looked at Hazel.

He did too and said, "I got it." He grabbed one of her braids and let it snake through his fingers just like Marco did that one time. "I'll see you later okay. Next time I'ma have something for you too."

Ready to get out, I hugged Hazel, and we walked out the door.

Once in his car he said, "I'm gonna get you another phone. I'm gonna teach you the ropes too. And I'm going to put you in touch with one of my good friends. She's like a sister to me. Her name is Angie...but they call her Angry Angie."

"Why?"

"You'll see," he laughed once to himself. "Anyway, I love the locs, but sometimes we gonna have to do your hair up in a wig and cover up them face tats. So that clientele will know you have variety. I'm gonna also get you some clothes. Because the better looking you are, the more money you get. Sure there's a market for trashy bitches too, but there's levels to this shit."

It was like I wasn't in the room. He just kept talking.

"But cheer up though," he adjusted his shades. "You skinny. So with the right backing, the proper makeup choices and some good shoes we can be on top."

"We," I said to myself.

I don't remember him telling me the part where he was gonna have to sell ass.

"I just gotta give you a name now." He looked me over for what felt like forever. And then a smile stretched in the corners of his lips. "Lemon...they will call you Lemon."

Lemon had been selling pussy for two weeks and already she had problems.

As she sat on the edge of a dingy comforter, legs crossed at the ankle and her phone rested face down on her thigh, she was thinking about getting out. The thought was short lived because she had no skills she felt could pay the bills. And so, there she was, in a motel that some of Giant's girls would go to see if they would get any requests for dates, waiting on the protégé's direction.

Angry Angie was light skin, skinny and way older looking than her age. The year of her birth said she was thirty-six, but she looked fifty-two if she was a day. It was whispered that her pussy was proper, but she had an attitude. Being smart on her feet she went into Doma matrix type of appointments, and her clients ate it up.

So despite getting Giant's girl's together, she too was also up for sale.

When she gave the other girls orders, she gazed at Lemon and lit a cigarette, squinting through a cloud of smoke. "You look like hell."

Lemon didn't flinch. "I've been feeling...off."

"Off how?"

"I don't know...like my body ain't mine."

"I need more."

"I been getting yeast infections...I stink...like I don't feel fresh, and I can't explain it."

"Any itching?"

"Nah...well sometimes."

Angie took a long drag and blew it toward the ceiling. "Your PH off," she said. "Happens to young hoes like you when you don't know what to do."

"But why?"

She shrugged. "Stress, diet, no rest, dehydration, too much friction and not enough care. That's the kind of life you stepping into."

Lemon leaned forward. "That's why I'm here. Help."

Angie raised an eyebrow. "You only had six clients so far and you fucked up already? A whore be at least on their twentieth before they fall apart."

"I'm not falling apart."

When she laughed cigarette smoke expelled her lips. "I mean...you sure you want this?"

Lemon opened her mouth, then closed it.

Angie stood up slowly, her joints cracking like old floorboards, and made her way over to a drawer stuffed with

86

crumpled papers and a bottle of cheap perfume. She pulled out a worn notepad and scribbled. "What you doing?"

"Writing you a list of things to get. So you better take heed."

Lemon was more curious than ever.

"How much water do you drink?"

Lemon shrugged. "None."

"Well if you ain't drinking water your pussy stinks."

"That's a lie. I never had any complaints."

"See that's the misconception. Before you were in this life you were a square. And a square has nothing to compare anything with but the square life. So let me be clear, the niggas you fucked may have bust, but if you not drinking water your pussy off and they knew it. Just never felt enough of you to let loose of the truth. Water flushes the system…puts things in order. Without it the toxins remain causing your odor to be off."

Just then another girl came, and Lemon remained on the bed feeling dumb until Angie told her where to go next. When the girl left with her new location, Angie commenced to frying her some more.

"So this is what you gonna do, stank cooch."

"Excuse me!"

"Drink Pedialyte…the clear kind to make the pussy wet and to keep toxins flowing. After a client busts, don't stay in bed with him...get up, go to the bathroom and push down as hard as you can on the toilet. You wanna push hard to get any remnants out, even with wearing a condom. Next wash up with an antibacterial soap, all over your body. After that clean with a feminine wash that has boric acid. Get the boric suppositories too, to keep your balance tight. Those go inside that funky tunnel. And if you aren't sure how fresh it is down there on any given day...get a pack of water-based baby wipes and pour witch hazel inside. Do not stick it in the pussy but wipe the lips and your hot spots. Kills the odors on contact. Now do you have a wet or dry pussy?"

"Normally dry unless I'm with my boyfriend."

"Well every nigga gonna be your boyfriend. This is the 304 life. Every man, and I do mean every man, needs to feel like it's a 304 love story. So I want you to take some slippery elm supplements...to keep it gliding. And to avoid them nasty looking bumps after shaving, get the High Rollers Topical to keep shit smooth."

She was writing on the pad like she was penning a novel.

"In between clients your drink of choice is fresh squeezed juice because it's real, you're going to take a sixty billion count probiotic and keep your skin moisturized with EOS lotion." She paused and looked around. "Oh...oh....and when you giving head put a mint strip on your tongue and let it

BY T. STYLES

melt. Because one of them niggas said your top game was trash."

"My top game was trash. I don't — ."

"You gotta complaint. Happens to the worst of y'all."

"But won't the strip burn them?"

Angie smiled like she had all the answers...because she did. "It will be the most exhilarating experience in their life. Trust me." She put down her pen.

"This a lot."

"This ain't a game, sweetheart," she whispered. "This ain't heels and money and glitter. It's spit in the mouth, bruises where nobody can see, and regulars who act like they own you. You probably thought you could walk into this like it's just a side hustle...but this shit changes people. And not always in a way you can come back from."

She ripped off the paper and handed it to Lemon.

"Here. If you're gonna be out here, your PH gotta be in check, your scent neutral, your mouth clean, your skin on point, and your energy even cleaner. These are the basics. Bare minimum. If you can't do these, you ain't built for this life."

Lemon looked at the list but didn't say anything.

"What about when I'm off for my cycle?"

"Ain't no days off. You get them makeup sponges, cut them to fit if you have to, and push them up there. They suck blood like vampires."

Lemon's throat tightened. She wanted to cry. In that moment she needed her mother…she needed another option. Maybe rolling with Giant was a mistake.

Angie sat next to her; arms crossed. "Listen here, bitch, if I was as young as you and could do it all over, I'd go the other fucking way. So don't be coming to me crying and shit because ain't no space for that here. Go find a job in somebody's dull-ass office. Flip burgers. Do hair. Anything else squares do."

"But I need money."

Angry Angie walked to the door and opened it wide. "Well your hoe ass betta get to work!"

The first man who responded to the social media page Giant helped me set up was a father. He'd actually just had a baby, and his wife couldn't have sex due to having to wait the necessary period. Still, the trick explained that he had to have sex every day, or he just wouldn't feel right.

So he ordered me.

I thought that was mean to his wife, but who was I to talk?

90 **BY T. STYLES**

And then stuff got weird. When we got into the room, instead of fucking me, he wanted to eat me out. Before I even got there he made sure to let giant know that he didn't want me to bathe or wash up in any capacity. It didn't matter if I had to shit. He wanted me just to wipe to get off the remnants and leave the rest.

When I got there, he ate me out so long my clit throbbed, and it was kind of painful. Only after going down for an hour did he raise up, put the condom on, and push inside me.

Luckily I didn't have to spend too much more time with him because he was quick.

My next trick was different.

He wanted things done in a particular way. I had to lay on my belly, reach for my ankles, and spread my legs in a way that he could see my pussy, pink and puttering.

I wasn't sure, but I had a feeling he was taking pictures.

I cried that day because he was rough and uncomfortable. But Giant didn't wanna hear it. He told me if I want to work, which I did, then I had better get comfortable with being uncomfortable.

I convinced myself he was right.

Before long I noticed something. I never got a lot of cash.

A few dollars here and there.

Where was the big money everybody talked about?

Every time I thought about stopping, Giant would take me out to eat, put me in a luxury hotel, and then do me right. At first, the hotels were bland, not top tier. But now I was in five stars all the way around.

I asked Angry Angie, since he had her giving me the ropes why he was doing what he was doing with the excursions.

She said, "If you knew how much money you were bringing in, you would have your answer."

Now I was angry, because if I was making that kind of money, he damn sure wasn't paying me. Every time I asked for more, he went into detail about how he needed to pay for my new clothes, my wigs and Angry Angie's consultation fee.

He said once that fee was paid I would get more and kept mentioning a marketing expense, which I was aware of having gone to school. But I also knew marketing fees were always a percentage not the full amount.

In other words, I should've seen way more money by now.

But I would soon find out how much I was earning.

And it would almost end my life.

BY T. STYLES

CHAPTER TWELVE

On a late but early morning, I came in with my shoes in my hand, trying not to wake anybody.

The front door creaked louder than I remembered, and the floor under the hallway rug gave a little groan that let the whole house know I was home. I closed it quietly behind me, stepped over the pile of sneakers by the wall, and tiptoed down the hallway.

The door to the room I shared with Hazel was cracked open and I pushed it wider. Hazel often left it like this when she wanted to be nosy to see who the neighbors were bringing in and out of their rooms.

But when I stepped inside, I saw the bed was made. Still neat.

But empty.

Hazel wasn't there.

My heart dropped into my stomach.

I turned around and walked fast to the kitchen where Sheree was standing by the stove, wearing one of her oversized T-shirts and favorite red bonnet still tilted to the side from sleep.

She didn't even look up.

"Where's Hazel?" I asked. "It's five in the morning."

Still, she didn't face me. Just flipped a piece of turkey bacon in the pan like this was any other morning. "She been out," she said.

"Been out. Out where?"

"With the wrong type. Although she's usually home by now."

That made me step forward.

"Sheree—"

She finally turned, greasy spatula still in hand, eyes sharp. "You wanna live this 304 life with that nigga Giant? Fine. But I'm not a mother and that little girl ain't built for this. Do not visit this type of responsibility on me. So if you want her to live here, you better do a better job of mothering her. But leave me out of it."

I swallowed hard, throat dry. "I didn't bring her into my lifestyle."

"You sure about that?"

I didn't wait for her to say more.

I left.

Started walking fast through the neighborhood, cutting corners and checking places I knew she'd hang out. The corner store with the dusty snack aisle, the basketball court with the half-torn net, the alley by the rec center where older kids gathered even when the streetlights came on.

Before long, I found her near the laundromat, sitting on a low brick wall talking to a boy.

He couldn't have been older than fifteen, hair twisted, sneakers bright, and he was laughing like she was the funniest thing in the world.

Hazel saw me before I said a word.

Her smile disappeared.

I didn't speak.

I just rushed her ass and reached for her hand.

She pulled it back, just for a second.

But I took it anyway.

Firm.

Not angry.

Just seriously.

"Come on," I said. "We not playing these games tonight. You just twelve."

"Twelve?" The boy said. "She said fourteen."

She didn't argue, but I felt her resistance in every step. I didn't look at the boy. He didn't say anything else either.

When we got back to the house, she walked ahead of me. Straight to our room before sitting on the edge of the bed, arms crossed tight.

"Why you always act like I'm doing something wrong?" She said, voice sharp, eyes glassy.

I didn't answer right away. Just sat across from her at the small desk in our room, elbows on my knees, heart still thudding from the fear I didn't want her to see.

"I'm trying, Hazel," I whispered. "Even when I'm messing up, I'm still trying. But you can't leave this house without me knowing where you are. I care about you. I don't wanna see anything happening to you."

Later that night, when we were both showered, she slept towards one wall, and I slept toward the other. I said, "Are you mad at me?"

"No. Because at least you care."

I smiled as I drifted off to sleep, and for some reason I felt she was smiling too.

CHAPTER THIRTEEN

I had perfected the art of selling pussy without selling pussy on social media. I never said the word ho'ing. But after a while, you knew what to say, and what not to say to let men know what you were into.

But it was my look that always worked in my favor.

My nails were always done, my locs were always twisted, and my makeup was on point.

I found that my clientele liked me with makeup, but not too much. A few told me they wanted to make sure I wasn't trans, so they needed to see my face. That was funny to me because I had come across so many trans women and most niggas didn't care or could tell whether they wore makeup or not.

Anyway, this particular night I was hired for a party.

Giant was excited and promised to take me out of town to get some new clothes so I could look the part. When it was all said and done, because of the money I was going to make, (he didn't tell me how much) he said we could splurge. So I got jewelry, shoes and even night wear so that my client would be impressed if he kept me the night.

I got the feeling when the car pulled up to the hotel I was staying in that whoever was paying for me, had big money.

We were in the Four Seasons and apparently there was also a party I was going to.

When I finally made it to the lobby, I walked up to the man in the red designer suit, no shirt. Just chiseled brown chest that looked as if he was dipped in shea butter. His name was Diamante, and he was an NFL player.

I was tripped out because he was so good looking he could have his choice. Why was he getting me through a pimp?

"You look beautiful," he told me.

"Diamante?" I said, extending my hand. He shook it softly. "Th…thank you. For the compliment."

"Right this way."

As he led me through the party he kept his hand on the lower part of my back. Surprisingly enough I was good at this shit. Maybe them college courses came in handy after all. I smiled at some people and held light convo with others. And for a moment I wasn't a 304, I was, dare I say, his lady. I learned later that he had paid for the entire night and I was happy because I didn't want it to end.

98

Everything seemed magical and it made it easy to sink into his world.

As Diamante and I found alone time he would stare at me, into my eyes and wipe a dread behind my ear. He was easy going...sweet...kind. Nothing like what I have been accustomed to.

"I like talking to you," he said as I took a sip from my red wine.

"I like that you enjoy speaking to me. And I like it for both of us."

"That's a different way of saying it." He chuckled. "You could be doing anything. I mean anything."

I knew what that meant. They all had the same comment. I was too pretty to be a whore, but if I wasn't then I wouldn't be with them for the night. "I understand. But for now I'm here."

When the last drinks were served, he kindly walked me toward the elevator and then his room. But instead of going right in he backed me against the wall next to his door. "I'm making more money than I ever have in my life."

I smiled. "I love that for you."

"You know what that makes me feel?"

"Tell me."

"Bored." He sighed. "What do you want from life, Lemon?"

For starters I wanted him to call me my real name. Jaystar. Other than that, I was almost too scared to answer his question. I had been doing this for over six months and nobody ever asked before. "I want to own my own business. That's what I was going to school for...business administration."

"Why didn't you finish?"

Silence.

"I got into a situation that I needed to help my mother out of."

"Your mother prevented you from going to college? No parent should ever move like that."

I didn't want to hate him, but I needed him not to be so judgmental against my mother. "Why do you ask? I mean...what I took up in college?"

"If you agree to be there when I need you, I'll set you up for life. I'm just going to need you to walk away from this shit. You could possibly even go back to school."

"But...why?"

"Because I can. And I'm not saying it will be forever, but it could be the jumpstart you need now."

I looked down and he picked my chin back up. "Head up, Jaystar. This is your chance."

100   BY T. STYLES

My heart rocked and my eyes widened. "How do you know my name?"

"When I left you earlier today, I had my assistant look you up. Before I even made this proposal. So you gonna take me up on it?"

"But...but he will be so mad."

"Fuck that nigga. You don't need him. He got other women. I've been with one before. Canceled her three hours later. So trust me when I say you're one of a kind."

"But...I..."

"How much you think I'm paying him for tonight?"

"I have no idea."

"Five grand. But I would've paid ten." He stepped closer. "So what you gonna do?"

Five grand? For me. The nigga Giant was stealing all my paper. "How do I know this ain't a game?"

"You don't."

"So why spend so much money on me?"

"How about you take a chance and find out?"

"I gotta think about it. Because I...I'm taking care of my next-door neighbor. Actually she's like a little sister to me. So where I go she would have to go too."

"That's not a problem for me if it ain't for you."

"I want to trust you...but I don't believe—."

"You don't believe you deserve the fairytale." He nodded. "Neither did I until I was drafted to play a game I worked at all my life."

"It's not the same."

"What if it is?" He said seriously. "You probably spent your entire life loving and wanting love. Am I right?"

He was.

"You're primed for this moment. Don't let Giant trick you out of a chance."

The last time I prayed I was in my mother's house. I can't see God answering me like this. But what if *He* did? "You don't love me."

"No...not yet...but I love who you are, and I'm telling you I don't have to lie to you. The fee has already been paid. What the real question at this moment is...what do *you* have to lose?"

When he said he was cool with Hazel I made a decision fifteen minutes later. "My answer is yes."

He smiled like he was genuinely happy. If this was a role-play, I didn't want it to end.

"And don't worry about your things. Chances are they not good enough for you anyway. We'll buy you and your little friend more stuff."

For the first time in months I was excited for the future.

We didn't even have sex. Just stayed up talking about my hopes and his dreams.

The next morning while we ate I called Hazel. She was home and I Door Dashed her some food. Me and Diamante also had breakfast. Pancakes, eggs and sausage. The coffee was tasty, and the orange juice was crisp and cold.

He must've saw my mind wandering because he assured me that things would be good every time I thought about what Giant might do. Even though Giant had done nothing violent, if I was making him as much money as people let on, would he so easily let me go?

A couple hours after breakfast, we had lunch, and it was two o'clock in the afternoon. At this point Giant called seven times, but there was no need for me to answer.

Diamante had already made phone calls and got me and Hazel a little place in Baltimore, that was anything but little. It was on the harbor, and I had windows in every room. He showed it to me on the phone, and the person told me they would be there to help me move in later that day.

Diamante had that kind of power.

Of course I let Hazel see the pictures and she already knew how she wanted her room to be decorated which made my heart light up with joy.

I didn't care if it was a game Diamante was playing.

I was willing to take the chance like I did every day since becoming a 304.

When it was time for us to go I stepped outside of the hotel and Diamante went back in to settle the bill. I was waiting on the curb for his car.

As I thought about how I would decorate our place, my mind wandered, and my feet moved. The valet smiled at me, probably seeing my joy. At the same time, what I would do for Hazel brought me more happiness than what I would do for myself. I wondered what I would tell people and how they would react.

It wouldn't matter though, because I had tasted the cool air for one moment before Giant pulled up to me in a Sprinter with two large men on each side. He stood in the center. "Get inside before I crack your jaw."

I shook my head no.

"If you make me lay hands on you, it won't end well. Now get in, hoe."

I obeyed.

I don't know what he knew, but I knew it must have been enough because the moment I got to the motel, he beat me in a way I didn't think I would ever recover from.

Kicks to the face.

Feet to the gut.

I was a small woman and trying to handle that much rage broke me inside and out.

It took me two weeks to heal and even then my arms wouldn't move the same whenever I tried to reach up. I would feel my bones crack and my back hurt greatly when it was cold. Hazel had the unfortunate job of helping me heal. But she never judged me. Just loved me. Even my cousin let me off easy by avoiding the *I told you so's*.

Although the dream was over, me and Hazel spent the days talking about living in our new place on the harbor and the nights talking about how it would soon be our life. We both knew it was make believe, but we didn't care. It felt good to dream instead of hurting.

Diamante called two times asking if I was sure I didn't want his help. I said I couldn't go. It would've been yes immediately but yesterday Giant asked me how Hazel was.

That was it. A silent threat.

So I told him it was still no.

But for a hoe, like me, I was grateful to even have him ask.

CHAPTER FOURTEEN

After healing from what Giant did to me I thought things would be good.

When another client beat me. It took me off guard because he was someone who I had been with in the past. It happened because I told him I was not doing anal, and he snapped. I dreaded going home because I knew Hazel would see me hurt again in the trust she had to be protected would be weakened.

The second I stepped through the door, Hazel saw the bruise and cried. Not a loud cry. But an audible one all the same.

I didn't even make it to the bed before her face changed. That look...the one that always hits deeper than anyone's words...pure sadness mixed with disappointment. Her eyes locked onto the side of my cheek, swollen and tender, just beneath my eye.

"Jay..." she whispered.

I tried to walk past her like it wasn't there. Like it wasn't pulsing, aching and turning purple beneath the concealer I didn't bother to reapply. But we were staying in a room with a bathroom, so the space was limited.

She stepped in front of me. "Why do you let them hurt you?" Her voice cracked. "You so nice...and pretty.

She was a kid, so I didn't want to talk about it. Besides, what did she know? "Leave it alone."

"You're always gone," she said. "And when you come back, you're different. And it scares me."

"I said I don't wanna talk about it." I walked past her and sat on the bed, untying my shoes with more force than needed.

She didn't move.

"I don't understand you anymore," she said. "You used to talk to me."

Did I say she was twelve?

My head snapped up because I was sick of this ungrateful shit. "You think I'm doing this for me?" I yelled. "You think I like being out all night? Getting bruised. Hiding what I do from people who wouldn't understand."

Hazel blinked, probably caught off guard.

I softened...just barely.

"So it's true. You're a 304 girl."

For some reason, the words coming out of her mouth hurt badly. It was the dirtiest I'd ever felt. "I'm doing this for you," I said. "So you don't end up like me. So you don't have to beg your way through life."

"But I don't want you to. I would rather…I would rather go back to my mother than to see you like this."

That ripped me deep. "You don't know what you saying. I'm good over here. Ain't shit changed."

Hazel shook her head, voice trembling. "Then why does it feel like I'm losing you?"

That hit harder than the fist that left my cheek swollen. She walked closer, her hands twisting in front of her. "Please stop," she said, barely above a whisper. "Maybe I can get a job and —"

"You're just a child and anyway it's not that simple." I looked away. Out the window. At the moon. At anything that wasn't her eyes. "I know what you want, Hazel, but I can't."

"What if this was me? Would you understand how I feel? How much I'm afraid."

I can't believe this girl is really only twelve.

"This will never be your life," I told her.

She didn't cry more.

She didn't yell.

She just turned her back to me, got in bed and laid down on her side. Quiet, still, and further away from me than she'd ever been.

CHAPTER FIFTEEN

Although time had passed since Giant hit me over Diamante, for some reason Angry Angie was still mad. I only knew this because of how many stupid mothafuckas she would call him about simple stuff in front of me.

Like when I came over to see if any clients were waiting and she'd say, "That stupid, black bastard, mothafucka sent you without telling me again?"

Or even the time I saw him Door Dash her some food and she would say under her breath, "That stupid mothafucka wants me to work for him longer. And I'm not having it."

All of this, and I do mean all, was out of character for their relationship. I learned from another hoe that she liked me, even though I couldn't tell. I guess she saw something in me that was once her. I only know this because she mentioned it several times.

I'm also sure she had a child out there somewhere because I heard her overtalking to a friend. When I brought it up she got defensive, and I never talked about it again.

BY T. STYLES

My thing was this, I hadn't forgotten about what Giant did to me. The only difference is now, since I knew he was violent, I had to be careful.

For me and Hazel.

So I decided I would no longer play stupid. If he was going to control my money, there was nothing I could do about it right now, but at least I would learn the game. Because even though he had been giving me one hundred here or there, he claimed I still owed due to my upkeep.

When Angry Angie was getting me ready for another high-profile client at the motel, she looked me in the eyes and said, "What you wanna know?"

"Huh?"

"What you wanna know about the game?"

She had a way of knowing when something was up with me. I don't know how, but she was always right.

Since she was asking I decided to take her up on her offer. "Months ago you said if I knew how much I was getting paid, then I'd be surprised. Well, how much are they paying for me?"

"Who's they?"

"Angie, you know what I'm talking about."

"I really shouldn't be telling you about this."

"I'm asking anyway."

She took a deep breath, brushed my hair back, and pulled it into a smooth ponytail. The client who'd selected me liked it that way. And I knew it was because he could pull on it when he was hitting me from behind.

To be honest, that was the only time I knew I was meeting with this particular trick. It was due to my hair. To even get this style right, my locs had to be smoothed and pulled so much I had Asian-like eyes. I didn't mind the hairstyle. I just minded the reason.

"He's paying about fifteen hundred for you."

Me knowing that he would only kick me about a hundred later incensed me. "Wow. That ain't what he giving me."

"You don't get more because you don't demand more. To be honest all the others get at least twenty percent. And they don't clock nearly as much as you do."

I officially hated him.

"How do I ask him for my money? I don't even know where to start."

"I can't help you with that part, Lemon. That's something you gonna have to work out on your own. But if you gonna survive, and help that little girl too, you better start thinking about it now."

Giant never takes me to my appointments, but I was glad he did this time because we had unfinished business to deal with. As he drove down the street, I glanced at him. "How long am I staying with this person?"

"I'll call you when it's time to leave."

"Why can't you just tell me?"

"Because he may want more time. But don't you worry about it because that's an arrangement I'll make with him."

He gripped the steering wheel with both hands, his tell for pretending to be focused so much I'd stop asking questions. But it wasn't working this time.

"How much are you getting for me?"

"What difference does it make?"

"How much?"

He glared at me, stared back at the road, then glared again. "Hold up. So you don't trust me?"

"So this is a trust issue just because I wanna ask about my money?"

"Your money? You still owe me."

I checked the dates on my phone that I had been on tricks. "I been on over three hundred dates. Some of them high profile. So you should be good with that marketing fee you charged by now."

"Hold up, you don't know what the fuck people pay me."

"Diamante kicked you over $5,000."

He glared. "I knew I couldn't trust that sucker for love ass nigga."

"So at this point, I know you've gotten well over the $3,700 you claimed I owed."

Silence.

"I don't understand why it's a problem that we talking about my money. If I'm putting in the work, I should get more in my hands."

"You know what?" He jerked the car onto the shoulder. "You think you can do this better than me?"

For a second, I just looked at him. I couldn't believe I trusted him in the first or second place.

"I don't know what you wanna hear, but I'm making more money than the others and I want a bigger cut."

"You know what? Get out, hoe."

I was dressed in tights, heels, a red halter top, and a jean jacket. Not to mention the ponytail smothering my natural locs. If I walked anywhere, I'd sweat everything off in an hour.

"You putting me out just because I'm asking for my money?"

"I said, get out!"

"This ain't fair."

"You want me to say it again?"

After what he'd done to me at the hotel, the last thing I wanted was a fight. So I opened the door. With that, I stepped out. The road ahead was long...real long but I was different now.

Nothing would be the same.

CHAPTER SIXTEEN

*H*azel had been saving for three weeks.

Every night Lemon came home late and slid a crumpled bill into her hand with tired eyes and a kiss on the forehead. It wasn't much but with every bill Hazel tucked a portion of it away. Just a few dollars here and there but it was enough to buy a bag of rice, some seasoned chicken from the corner store or a box of cornbread mix that she used during her scheduled time in the community kitchen inside Sheree's house.

But today was very different and she wanted to share it with Lemon.

The entire process was an event for the twelve-year-old.

She cleaned the whole room before she started cooking. Lit one of Sheree's old candles and sat their mismatched bowls side by side like it was a restaurant and not just a rented room in someone else's house.

When she heard the door creak open, she smiled with excitement.

Finally. She couldn't wait to surprise her friend.

But the second Lemon stepped inside, Hazel saw her bad mood. Despite the nasty disposition, Hazel felt she looked pretty with her ponytail hanging to the back. Still, Lemon's face was tight as she dropped her bag on the bed without looking around.

"Hey," Hazel said, softly. "I made something. For us."

Lemon glanced at the table.

Steam rose gently from the plate.

"Hazel, I can't right now," she said. "I need to make some calls because a lot changed."

Hazel's smile washed away. "But...I was waiting all night and — "

"I said I can't. Now I won't do this shit with you today. With the million fucking questions."

Lemon didn't mean to snap, but it came out sharp and hard, the way things do when you're carrying too much and someone dares to tug on your sleeve.

Poor Hazel stood frozen, blinking fast. "It's my birthday, bitch!"

The words hit the room like a dropped plate. The girl may have cursed but any fool could see it was out of pain.

Lemon had been flinging pussy so hard, she failed to remember the day the child was born. Sure she kept the date in her mind on many occasions when they were neighbors. But now, well now it totally missed her.

"I didn't want anything big," Hazel whispered. "I just wanted to eat with you."

Lemon looked up slowly, as if the words were still sinking in.

Hazel didn't wait. She turned and ran out the door, her footsteps too fast to be caught by a mean whore in heels.

After looking through the house for Hazel, Lemon reentered the room and flopped down on the chair. The weight of guilt pushing into her chest like a stone.

The candle on the table still flickered and one of the cornbread squares had already started to cool and crack at the edges.

After claiming she cared so much for Hazel, she didn't even know what day it was.

Giant consumed so much of her energy that she didn't know what mattered anymore outside of money, survival and the hustle. Her whole life had become one long scramble forward, and somewhere in the blur, she had forgotten how to stand still.

But there was one man who watched from the shadows.

He always watched.

And he would use this moment to his advantage.

BY T. STYLES

Hazel wiped her cheeks on her sleeve as she rounded the corner of the block.

She didn't know where she was going. Just that it hurt to be inside with Lemon. After walking aimlessly, she sat down on a low curb near the alley and pulled out her phone. No missed calls.

Until there was one.

Giant.

She hesitated because she already forgot he asked, and she gave him her number. He claimed it was for emergencies, in the event something happened to Lemon. But then he told her not to let Lemon know which seemed odd.

Curious now though, she picked up. "Happy birthday," he said, voice like velvet, slow and certain.

Hazel blinked. "...You knew?"

"Of course I did," he said. "You think I would forget a birthday like yours? One that important to me. I even got something for you."

Her face lit up.

Just a little.

"Really?"

"Mmhmm, hmmm. You want me to give it to you? Or do you still want me to stop calling like you told me earlier?"

When he called some time back and tried to talk on the phone she yelled at him. Told him not to be weird. But now things had changed.

She felt betrayed by her best friend.

To make matters worse, she looked around and saw Lemon nowhere. Maybe she was done fighting for her after all. She didn't know Lemon had walked earlier to get her car, and that her feet still hurt too much to move quickly. "No...you can call me now."

"Well tell me where you are. Let's not waste more time." After giving him the info the call ended, she stared at the screen for a moment, her smile lingering a bit too fucking long.

CHAPTER SEVENTEEN

I was halfway out the door to go look for Hazel for the fourth time when Sheree's voice cut through the hallway like a slap in church. "Jaystar."

I stopped, hand on the knob, still halfway in my own head. "What?"

She stepped out the kitchen, arms folded, yellow towel still slung over one shoulder from cleaning. "The kitchen dirty."

I shook my head. "I haven't used your kitchen."

"You haven't, but your friend did."

I thought about the meal she made for us. Damn I wished she would've cleaned it. And then I remembered it was her birthday.

"I let you rent that room 'cause you family," she continued. "And because you pay on time. But I didn't sign up to be nobody's babysitter."

I blinked at her. "Babysitter?"

"I'm talking about Hazel."

My stomach twisted. "Can you fucking relax? Every day you at me about some shit pertaining to that girl."

Sheree let out a breath like she'd been holding it in too long. "She been keepin' time with niggas. Not one.

Not two. Multiple. I don't care if they just holding hands or fucking, it's too much, especially if she sneaking them in here."

"Sneaking them in here."

"I had to put them out, twice. And every time, she waits for me to go upstairs, and lets 'em back in."

I shook my head. "She—she wouldn't—"

"She has. Jay, you might not be raising her officially, but that little girl moves when you move. She looking at you to set the line."

"She's a kid."

"Exactly," Sheree said. "Which is why you gotta check her now, before you blink, and she turns into something you didn't plan for. You think I'm sayin' all this 'cause I don't like her? I'm sayin' it 'cause I been her."

I looked away. "I'll talk to her."

Sheree just shook her head. But I didn't have time to argue. Instead I waved her off and slipped out the front door, letting it close softly behind me.

The air outside was humid and thick. I started down the block on foot, which still hurt since Giant put me out earlier. My hope was that maybe Hazel had gone to that corner store she liked, or maybe she was around back, near the busted fence where we used to sit and make up stories.

I was maybe five houses down when my phone buzzed.

An unknown number.

I knew what that meant.

I stared at it for a second, thumb hovering. My breath caught.

Then I answered.

His voice was low, familiar, and all business. A new client. Good money. Wanted to meet tonight.

Right now.

I looked up the street, heart torn between the promise of fast cash and the girl who might be out here barefoot or worse.

Just a few hours. That's what I told myself.

Just long enough to take care of what needed taking care of then I'd be back.

I turned around slowly, phone still pressed to my cheek. "Text me the address."

The second I hung up, I felt it.

That tiny crack in my chest.

Hazel was somewhere out here.

And I was choosing money again.

Only God knew where she was.

But I knew exactly where I was headed.
And I hated myself for it.

BY T. STYLES

CHAPTER EIGHTEEN

*H*azel sat on the worn cement steps of an apartment building, arms folded across her chest, gently rubbing her forearms. The breeze was light but cold, brushing against her skin like a warning. She wore jeans and a snug pink short-sleeved shirt which was cute but not made for chilly nights like this. She looked small sitting there...waiting for the worst kind of man to enter her life.

Then, the deep growl of an engine broke the stillness.

A black, wide-bodied Benz rolled around the corner, its headlights slicing clean through the dark. Hazel's eyes lit up the second it slowed to a stop at the curb. The sleek black paint gleamed, and the chrome rims spun down slowly, like even the car didn't want to stop shining.

Within seconds, the driver's door opened, and there he was.

Giant.

He looked like money. Like the kind of man people followed without asking questions.

As he approached the thirteen-year-old, he moved with confidence...jeans perfectly tailored, a fresh white tee stretched over his chest beneath a jet-black bomber jacket. A thick gold chain glinted at his neck, and despite the night, he wore dark shades like they were a part of his skin.

The way he walked around to the passenger side and opened the door made him look like a rap star stepping out for a red-carpet moment.

She had seen him before but now she was awestruck.

The devil had a way of appealing to the vanity in people.

She stood up, heart racing, brushing her hands over her jeans without thinking. Slowly she stepped toward the car and slipped into the passenger seat. The scent inside was all leather and cologne, rich and warm, like something only expensive people could afford.

"You good?" Giant asked, his voice low and slick.

Hazel nodded; her eyes wide as she touched the smooth panel of the door.

"I'm takin' you somewhere special for your birthday," he said, pulling off with one hand on the wheel. "I hope you don't mind."

She grinned instantly, excitement fluttering in her chest. "Okay. Is that what you had for me?"

"What you talking about?"

She frowned. "You said you had something for me earlier."

He had gotten caught. "Oh...oh yeah. I was talking about taking you somewhere to let you cop your own shit. Wanna know where we going?" He asked glancing her way.

She shook her head, eyes on the dashboard lights. "No," she said. "I trust you."

He smiled having heard exactly what he fucking wanted to hear.

And so the grooming had begun.

Every designer she dreamed about, Giant made possible. Gucci. Prada. Saks. Hazel picked out jackets, jeans, two dresses, one pink, and a few pair of designer sneakers she couldn't stop staring at. Then came the prize...a tiny Louis Vuitton handbag. She clutched it with both hands like it was the key to a new life. She knew her friends were going to be sick when they saw it because she was never the girl with the labels.

She was now.

But the night wasn't over. Because after shopping, he took her out to eat.

The restaurant had dim lights and quiet R&B music playing in the background. Giant ordered like he owned the place, and Hazel followed suit, getting lobster, steak, and dessert without hesitation. The girl had no idea that the evening's meal was courtesy of Lemon's fuck game or that it would come with consequences. She was just happy to be in the moment. Her smile stretched wide across her face, full of joy and disbelief as she tasted the food.

"I think I could fall in love with you, young Hazel," he said suddenly, watching her from across the table.

Hazel blinked, caught off guard, the fork pausing halfway to her mouth.

"You don't have to say it back," he added. "Just know I'm gonna give you the world. But you gotta trust me. Over everybody else."

She looked at him seriously, voice soft. "That's easy."

He raised a brow. "Yeah? Why's that?"

"Because I don't got nobody," she said.

"What about Lemon?" He asked, the question sharp but delivered smooth.

Hazel hesitated, then shook her head. "No. Not even her."

Giant leaned back, his smile slow and knowing. Hazel didn't see the shift in his eyes.

But it was there.

And it spoke volumes.

BY T. STYLES

Hands full of bags, Hazel crept through the front door as quietly as she could, easing it shut behind her with a gentle click.

The room was dim, lit only by the soft glow of the hallway light spilling inside. She held her breath as she stepped across the floor, the weight of her new gifts making her heart pound with a thrill she couldn't contain.

One by one, she unloaded the shopping bags. A jacket still crisp with tags. A soft sweater that smelled like the boutique it came from. The tiny Louis Vuitton bag, her favorite, nestled on top of it all. But it was a pink dress that really caused her to pause. She stuffed her clothing deep into the closet, behind old boxes and a laundry basket full of clothes she hadn't touched in weeks. She didn't want Lemon to see.

Not until she figured out what to say. At the same time she wasn't her mother. So what of it if she had new gear?

Walking to the bathroom, the light flicked on and steam soon filled the air.

Hazel took a long shower, scrubbing the memory of the evening into her skin. When she stepped out, she towel-dried and carefully lathered on her favorite strawberry-scented lotion from Bath & Body Works, the smell sweet and sticky like candy. With the man still on the mind, she ran her hands down her arms, breathing it in, feeling new, like the version of herself she always wanted to be.

LEMON 129

He hadn't touched her and already she was open.

Slipping into a pair of pajama shorts and an oversized t-shirt, she crawled into bed, feeling like she hit the lotto. She wasn't used to shit so this would live rent free in her mind...for now anyway.

Once tucked deep, she reached for her phone, fingers tapping out a soft text, "Thank you for tonight 🖤."

The message sent, and she placed the phone gently on the pillow beside her. That's when she heard it...a car engine idling just outside the house.

Her smile faded slightly.

Head turned toward the window.

Lemon?

Quickly, she rolled onto her side, tugged the covers up to her shoulders, and closed her eyes. She let her breathing slow and deepen, trying to mimic sleep.

BY T. STYLES

CHAPTER NINETEEN

I was done with my client and kissed him on the cheek as I stepped out the hotel room. The hallway was quiet, the scent of stale cologne and cleaning supplies hanging in the air. The soft ding of the elevator echoed as I pressed the button, clutching my phone in my hand, thumb hovering over Hazel's name, I called her again.

Voicemail.

Called again.

Nothing.

But when I opened my room's door she was there. Faking sleep. All I felt was relief. And to be honest after missing her birthday I didn't deserve much grace.

I still had work to do because I wanted forgiveness so bad.

If only I knew how much trouble would come our way after this one incident, I would've quit the game all together.

The next day I was outside, and I knew I wanted to celebrate her right but she wasn't answering the phone. I decided to call Sheree's cell even knowing she would curse me out.

My heart was already picking up speed, but when Sheree answered, I felt a flicker of relief, until she spoke. "Can you go check on Hazel to make sure she in the house?"

"Jaystar, what did I tell you? I'm not your babysitter."

"I know, but—"

She didn't even let me finish. "You chose this life...now live in it."

The line went dead, and so did my hope of keeping anything in order tonight.

I should've gone straight home, but guilt wrapped around my neck like a scarf. Instead, I drove toward the bakery.

When I placed the order yesterday, after Hazel ran out, I figured it was a move in the right direction. It was Hazel's favorite, strawberry shortcake with extra whipped icing and pink roses piped along the top.

There was a problem. The place closed soon, so I glanced at the dashboard clock.

9:15 p.m.

They closed at 10. I dialed their number. "We have your cake," the girl on the other end said, her voice dry and uninterested. "It's boxed. Just like you asked. But we close at ten. So good luck getting here in time."

She hung up before I could respond.

Thanks for nothing.

I made a mental note never to use them again.

Back in my car, I was five minutes out when steam hissed up from the hood. A loud pop followed, and my car began to crawl like it was holding its breath.

Fuck! I pulled over.

The air outside was thick and sticky as I stepped out, immediately regretting the little red skirt and tank top combo I had on. It had served me well with the client, but out here? It was an invitation I never meant to send.

The ignorance from niggas was high.

"*Hey, baby, you need a real man to fix that?*" One said.

"*Lemme take a look under your hood so I can play in that pussy, baby.*" Yelled another. That one wasn't even fucking original.

I rolled my eyes, kept my back to them, and popped the hood myself. The steam hit me in the face like a punishment as I stared at the engine.

Black and metal and meaningless because at the end of the day I didn't know what the hell I was doing.

LEMON 133

Frustrated, I slammed the hood closed and stood on the edge of the road. A few cars passed and then a few more.

Then something inside me shifted.

I hadn't prayed in months. Maybe longer. But I lowered my eyes and whispered silently: God, I'm trying, and I know I don't deserve You. I just want to make Hazel's life better than mine. And I know I've made some messed-up choices, but please...if You can help me...just this once...I would appreciate it so much.

Not even sixty seconds later, a white minivan pulled over and an older black woman rolled down her window. Her kid sat in the back, eating from a bag of fast food. She said, "You okay, sweetheart? Because it's dangerous out here."

"No...no I'm not," I said trying to suppress a cry. "I just need to get to the bakery up the street. It's for my little sister's birthday."

The woman nodded. "Hop in. But I can't wait long."

"You don't have to. I just need to pick it up before they close."

Once inside, she drove fast, like a mom on a mission. I appreciated her for that shit. Before long we pulled up at the bakery at 9:59 p.m. and they were literally locking the door.

Pleading with the world for more time, I jumped out and pressed my watch to the glass, mouthing, I made it. They hesitated at first before they opened the door. Good for them because I had intentions on breaking every window in this bitch if they played games.

I believe she knew it and didn't want to come back the next day to trouble.

When the cool air smacked my face, moments later I walked out with the cake in hand, heart beating like it was a part of a drum line. And when I finally got to the house, just like last night I noticed the room was dark and she was home.

So why hadn't she answered my call?

Hazel was lying on her side, the curve of her back to me, eyes shut. I decided to speak to her instead. "I bought your favorite. For your birthday. And I'm so sorry for how I talked to you when you made dinner for me."

Silence.

"Hazel..." I whispered. "I know I been doing a lot. But I swear I have a plan. And one of these days you'll believe me."

She didn't move. Didn't blink.

I didn't expect her to.

With the uneaten cake on the desk, I changed out of my clothes and showered. Once clean I slid on a T-shirt and shorts.

When I heard her soft snoring I knew she was really sleep.

As I moved around, I caught her phone light up on the nightstand. But it was the name that flashed back that caused me to feel faint.

Giant.

My breath caught in my chest.

Fuck was he doing hitting her up? I wanted to wake her up so bad I couldn't breathe. Had I not messed up with her birthday I would not have cared. She would be rubbing her eyes and telling me what was going on.

But I did fuck up, so right now, I didn't say a word.

But tomorrow?

I had mothafucking questions!

When I opened my eyes, the first thing I noticed was the silence. The kind that didn't feel peaceful...it felt...wrong.

BY T. STYLES

Hazel was gone!

What the fuck? I had dreamed of what I was going to say to her and everything. All for nothing.

Normally, I wasn't a heavy sleeper. Years of looking over my shoulder made sure of that with Marco lurking around. But between the weight of last night's client and the tension with Hazel, I must've passed out harder than I expected. At the same time this wasn't over. Besides, we had to talk about Giant.

The side of the bed she normally curled into was cold and flat. And when I looked toward the small nightstand, my stomach dropped even more.

The cake.

Still in its box. Still perfect. Still uneaten. The pink frosted roses I rushed across town to get hadn't moved. Not one petal disturbed.

I sat up slowly, my muscles stiff and my chest heavy.

Where the hell are you, Hazel?

She hadn't left a note, hadn't texted. And after everything I went through…after everything we'd been through; I couldn't help but feel…hollow. After all, she's only thirteen. Sure she's the legal age to watch herself since it was over eight in Maryland. But she's still a child in my eyes.

And a child had no business keeping time with a man. Nobody knew that more than me, which made things all the more scary.

I don't usually snoop. It ain't my thing because I hate when people go through my shit, so I try not to violate. But something in me was pulsing…this sick, gnawing feeling and I needed answers.

So I went searching for them.

I started at her side of the bed. Pulled open the little drawer she kept jammed with random teenage nonsense…stickers, rubber bands, a broken charger, a mini bottle of cheap perfume, and half a chocolate bar still in its foil.

Nothing was out of the ordinary.

Then I went to the bathroom. Loose strands of hair were in the sink again. Long, curly strands that stuck to the porcelain like threads of evidence. And some were on the tile too…something I told her repeatedly to clean up. But there was no real clue here. Just hair. Just mess.

Then I moved to the closet.

As soon as I opened the door, I felt it.

Something was off. Things looked fuller…richer in color.

My fingers brushed fabric I didn't recognize. Tags still dangling. Shirts from stores I know damn well I never took her to. Jackets still crisp and folded, like they came from some luxury boutique. There were new shoes too...three pairs lined up neatly like they were waiting for approval.

My breath caught in my throat.

Labels. Expensive ones.

I stood there, frozen, one hand still resting on the hanger bar, trying to steady myself. My skin felt hot all of a sudden. And only one name came to mind.

Giant.

With shaking hands, I snatched my phone and did something I told myself I would never do again after he put me out of his car, forcing me to kick rocks on foot. I dialed his number.

No answer.

Called again.

Still nothing.

A third time...voicemail.

I paced, phone in my hand, rage rising in my chest. It was one thing to use me. I walked into that deal with my eyes open. But Hazel?

A newly aged thirteen-year-old.

No wonder he didn't try to get me to come back. He had stolen Hazel's mind and knew I would come begging on hands and knees.

I was going to get to the bottom of it. I was going to burn this whole bitch down if I had to. But first...I had a client waiting.

And I needed the money —

To get us the fuck out of the city.

I also realized I was in over my head, and I needed my cousin more than ever if I was going to help Hazel.

It was time to relent and really listen to what she had to say. I told you so's and all.

BY T. STYLES

CHAPTER TWENTY

Since me and my cousin were always in her house I decided we should meet somewhere else. When I called her I learned she was at her boyfriend's crib, so we decided to meet in front of his apartment building.

As I parked the car I just got fixed, I peeped something I hadn't noticed before. Prior to working for Giant, people used to overlook me.

I don't know if my body changed although I did gain five or six pounds, but men seemed to look harder. And if I do say so myself, I gained the weight in the right places. I had not only learned the art of seduction but had become a seductress.

Later for all that…it was time to get serious.

When I walked up on her Sheree crossed her arms over her chest and tilted her head. I guess bracing for the worst.

"Hey," was the first thing I said. Now that I think about it, it sounded dumb, but I had to start somewhere.

"*Hey?*" She responded. "That's all you say to me after calling my phone like you crazy. Like you couldn't wait to tell me in the house."

I took a deep breath. "I've been moving in ways I'm not proud of. But I'm about to pause a little."

"And what exactly does that mean?"

"I'm not fucking with Giant no more."

"Is this your choice or his?"

"Does it matter? I'm going to move without him, until I can stack some paper and pay up my room rent for a year, whether I'm living there or not. And I need your help."

"Why would you wanna do that? Like pay that far in advance."

"Because whether I'm there or not, I need a safe place for Hazel to rest her head."

"I told you I'm not a babysitter. So what you want me to do? Get—."

"Custody," I said nodding slowly, feeling like I wanted to cry. "If something happens to me I want you to get custody." Next I pulled out my phone and showed her the life insurance policy I paid for earlier that day which was in her and Hazel's name.

"Wow, you serious about her."

"So can you promise me you won't throw her out? At least until she's eighteen."

It took a moment, but she said, "I promise."

"Okay, so I need your help with my tricks."

"If you think I'm going to be involved in some kind of freaky—"

"No," I said, cutting her off. "I don't expect you to be involved in what I do. I just need your help watching my back while I'm out. Since I don't have Giant no more. And with the exception of Angry Angie, who still on his roster, you the only one I know who knows the streets."

"I'm not about to let you sell yourself like—."

"I know you selling pussy, Sheree. We can tell every time you working because you light a candle in the house. And that's the real reason you worried about Hazel."

Silence.

"Are you going to help me or not?" I asked.

I love my cousin, but all the third-degree shit she was giving me was annoying at best because I knew she was selling pussy just like me. So she could either help or get the fuck up out my way. In both instances, the choice was hers.

"Okay," she said.

I leaned in just as a boy walked by and asked for my number. He was cute. And back in the day, I would've loved to give it to him. Just for a little attention. But that type of time was the least of my worries, so I sent him on his way.

"I'm gonna help and you're gonna pay me my fee too. Over and above whatever you stacking for rent."

"But what about the insurance policy?"

"You not dead yet, bitch. So I want my money now."

I laughed. Not because she wanted money, but because she had no problem asking for compensation for her time. I wish I had been that way. Maybe then I wouldn't have fell in Giant's trap for so long and Hazel would be safe.

I hadn't even planned to walk past our old building.

Besides, I wasn't sure what I was looking for, to be honest. Maybe a glimpse of the life that once made sense. Maybe it was just to find Hazel.

And then my world was rocked.

My chest ached, even before I spotted her walking up the steps to the apartment. She disappeared inside without my interruption. I hadn't spoken to my mother since everything happened. The silence between us was its own kind of bruising and it stung every time I breathed.

144

I was being overstimulated because then I saw Hazel.

She was leaning against the low brick wall out front, talking to a girl we used to see on the stairwell, back when we were both under the same roof. She was laughing, tossing her hair like she was older than she had any right to be. And in her hand?

A damn Louis Vuitton purse.

Tiny, but real.

She looked like a teenager trying to be a woman. That was the problem...she didn't just look like it. I could tell she believed it.

I took a breath so deep it burned my throat before moving slowly in her direction. "Can I talk to you for a minute?" I asked as I walked up, trying to keep my voice calm.

Gentle. Definitely different from how I addressed her when she first stopped talking to me.

"Hazel, I said can we talk?"

She rolled her eyes. Not even a full glance my way. Like I was just some woman on the street. Like I didn't make a home for her, and we didn't share the same bed.

But her friend, Leslie, who had always liked me, gave me a sympathetic smile. "Maybe you should talk to her and call me later. Jay's always been nice," she said before disappearing inside my building.

I appreciated that.

Now alone, Hazel stared past me like she didn't care what came next. But I had to try. "Listen," I said, stepping a little closer. "I'm sorry I forgot your birthday."

She shook her head, arms crossed so tight over her chest it looked like she was hugging herself. "What you want?"

I swallowed. "I want you to know that even though I forgot, I'm always thinking about you. Even when I'm out doing whatever I gotta do in the streets."

"You don't got to do nothing. You want to."

The hurt in her eyes was covered by attitude, but I saw through it.

"But you have to listen to me," I went on, my voice low but firm. "You can't have anything to do with Giant."

She flinched. Subtle. Barely there.

Yeah, this nigga had his grips into my friend.

"What are you even talking about?" She said. "I mean you rapping and rapping but nothing makin' since." She was doing puppet mouth with her fingers.

Fuck was that?

She had never done that before.

I couldn't get out of character because my spirit told me that's what she wanted. An excuse to cut me off forever. "I saw his name on your phone."

She shrugged. "And?"

"And you can't be messing with him," I said, trying not to shake. "You're a child, Hazel. And he will use you. Drain everything from you until there's nothing left."

The sky cracked above us. Thunder rolled so loud; it vibrated through my sneakers.

Hazel's eyes flashed. "You know what I think?"

Silence.

"I think you're jealous," she said.

My heart sank. "Jealous. Jealous of what?"

"You jealous that he likes me now. Not you. He told me this would happen."

The words hit me like a punch to the chest. Cold and hard and unexpected.

She believed it. That's what broke me the most.

I stepped forward. "If you gonna be staying with me," I said slowly, "then you gotta cut him off. Because trust me I'm having none of it."

"I'm not staying with you."

I blinked. "What?"

"I'm staying with my mother now."

I felt the ground tilt.

"You can't live with your mother," I reminded her. "You know she's gonna go back to her old ways. She already has. And all those new clothes you got? She'll sell them the first chance she gets."

"That's still my mother," Hazel snapped. "And she's more loyal to me than you. So just leave me the fuck alone."

"I won't leave you alone."

She swung her recently Brazilian pressed hair. "But you should though."

"Then I'll tell your mother you fucking with an older man. At thirteen." The moment I said it I felt like shit because I was betraying her trust. "I'm sorry. I won't do that but—."

She turned to walk away.

I took one step forward, stopped myself from grabbing her arm. "I don't care if you ever like me again, I'm not done fighting for you," I said, the words catching in my throat. "If you're happy here, with her, then fine, but I'll ask you every day in case you change your mind. And I'll leave your cell phone on too."

She paused but didn't turn.

"But when I'm sure it's what you want, I'm moving," I continued. "A townhome. I'll be there in a month, and I'll text you the address. If you ever need a place, if you ever want to come back…there'll be a key waiting."

CHAPTER TWENTY-ONE

I was motivated as fuck.

My cousin Sheree set up twelve clients for me, straight from social media. The first one was known for having deep pockets. The second client was his friend, and the third and fourth came through word of mouth.

Within two weeks, with Sheree's help, I had saved up $10,000 and I was still stacking. That's not including the money I gave her to keep a room for Hazel.

I was moving different though. I had made up my mind: I wouldn't accept just any invitation. If you wanted my services, you had to meet certain criteria.

1. You couldn't pay me less than my asking rate, which was $500.

2. You had to pay for my hotel of choice, usually a four-star hotel in Baltimore where nobody would suspect what I was doing. The same was for out-of-town visits too which I started to accept.

3. You had to have a phone number I could call back and some kind of presence either on social media or you'd have to show me your driver's license.

BY T. STYLES

Let's just say my pool of clients got smaller when I started asking for all that shit. I let them cover the address, but some people still had a problem with it.

I didn't care.

This was my way or no way.

My only exception and I do mean only, was if someone gave a personal referral.

For some reason, as time went on, I was feeling empowered.

I hadn't heard anything bad about Hazel, so I hoped she was doing well with her mother. It didn't matter though. Because when she needed me I would be there. I was earning my own money, doing my own thing, and I even helped my cousin Sheree set up her house the way she wanted.

I felt less stressed and hopeful, until I came in contact with what could only be described as a serial killer.

After him, my life changed dramatically.

CHAPTER TWENTY-TWO

He seemed too nice...very nice.

But this was an out-of-town client who had...a referral.

And so, I trusted him. He didn't want me telling anybody we were meeting, and he also wanted to be in control of where I stayed.

When I asked him why, preparing to deny him, he showed me pictures of him in office as a politician. At the same time, I needed my security, especially with being in Atlanta but knowing he was in the government made me a little easier.

Luckily I had Sheree, who had also flown in, although she didn't come with me. She flew separately to give the illusion that he was getting what he wanted. My isolation.

Other than that, he met all of my criteria.

He had a strong online presence as a politician. And when he picked me up from the airport, I was able to check his driver's license, and his name matched. Everything seemed okay except one thing.

He looked a little different than his pictures.

BY T. STYLES

Not in a bad way. In a good way. But I shouldn't have let my guard down.

He was over six feet tall, dark-skinned, and extremely attractive. But when I got to the hotel, I knew the day would be anything but ordinary. For starters, my reservation wasn't listed. Despite me confirming it before I arrived.

They assured me it wasn't cancelled but something had to happen.

I had definitely reserved it, even though he'd given his credit card, so I didn't understand what the problem was. To make matters worse, there were no other rooms vacant which meant my cousin was out.

The only room available was the room he reserved in his "fake name". I felt like that was off and didn't make since. Luckily he said he would not use it and arranged for me to pick up the key. In other words, my room wasn't available but the one in his fake name was, which he let me use.

If I was home it would be a no go. But I was there...so I tried to make things work.

He claimed he was picking me up for a party and that once I settled in, I should await a car to come get me. When the event was over, the plan was to come back to my room and finish my appointment, sexually.

So I called Sheree, and she said she was fine staying at a three-star hotel not far away. I would've gone there too, to get dressed, but it gave me the creeps. I'd had bad experiences with that hotel before and didn't want to risk something happening again.

My cousin said she didn't care.

When I was dressed I got in a chauffeured limo and was taken to a beautiful home in Buckhead, an upscale community near Atlanta. As I sat in the backseat I felt like it was a neighborhood built for stars. The evening was starting to not be so bad after all.

Was this his home?

And where was the party? Because outside of the limo I saw no other cars. Where was his? Maybe it was in the six-car garage.

The moment we pulled into his circular driveway he rushed out to open my door and for some reason, I felt at home.

It's amazing what money can do.

Once inside, he said, "Where is your purse? I'll take it."

Weird.

"That's okay...I can hold it."

He nodded and examined me fully. "You're perfect." Next he stood in the middle of the foyer before touching my elbow gently and led me to a large kitchen.

"Thank you...but...uh...where is everyone? For the party."

"I decided I wanted us to be alone."

My heart dropped.

"Do you want something else to eat?"

I nodded. "Why didn't you tell me about the change?"

"I'm telling you now." He smiled, showing me both rows of teeth. "So what do you want to eat?"

"I don't care." I put a hand on my belly to calm myself.

Why was I so nervous?

He whipped up something quick: a small salad, a chicken breast, and some white rice with garlic butter. The meal was modest but very tasty.

When we were done, he looked at me. "You're prettier than I imagined."

He already complimented my looks, and I wished he stopped with the extra shit.

Besides, I didn't know whether to take that as a compliment or an insult. I decided to be chill because I knew something was off. "Thank you," I told him. "Is this your house?"

"Yes. Are you ready?"

His response was short, and it gave me the creeps. But I figured, what's the worst that could happen? Then I remembered, Sheree didn't know where I was. Things had happened so strangely that I lost reason and contact.

So a lot could go wrong.

"We going back to the hotel?"

"No...I arranged for everything to end here."

End here?

"Uh...so where are we going in the house?"

"Give me a few minutes," he said as he walked away.

I used the time to contact my cousin Sheree. But when I tried to make a phone call, I had no service. In fact, just looking at my phone, there was no signal. Not for the internet, not for my apps, and definitely not for texting. Glancing out the window I saw the limo that brought me was gone.

I was all alone.

When he returned, he touched my elbow again. "Right this way."

I swallowed a little. "I can't make a phone call."

He shook his head. "I'm sorry about that. These old stone houses block reception. I'll check on the Wi-Fi later and give you the code."

I wanted to be at ease. "Can I have the code now?"

"No."

Let's just say he never gave it to me. But I did get something else.

I was naked on the bed, a rope tied to my wrist and the bed post on both sides of my body. My feet were also bound to the far end bed post. Just so we're clear, I didn't consent to this shit.

And yet there he was, on top of me. Sweaty and heavy. I tried to push him off but was unable. Why couldn't I get him off of me?

I decided to speak to him calmly. "Listen, you don't have to do this. I'm willing to—."

He hit me with the hardest right I had ever experienced in my life. The blow was so crucial it made me forget momentarily where I was. And when I tried to speak again, my mouth flooded with blood causing me to almost choke.

Horrified, I looked at him and his eyes were black as coal. He felt darker than he had earlier, and it made it more sinister when he started pumping in and out of me again.

"Please don't do this," I cried softly.

He didn't seem to care. In fact, when I tried to speak again, he grabbed my neck and squeezed, removing the breath from my lungs.

When I came to, he was sitting on the edge of the bed, yoga style, looking at me like I was a science project. He wore no clothes. Balls limp and touching the mattress. His dick hard and shiny though.

As my lids fluttered, he looked surprised. He didn't know I would survive. I could tell.

"You can handle it I see," he said with a grin. "But you going to find out how much tonight."

I didn't understand why I couldn't see him fully. I would later learn that my eyes were so swollen, liquid would have to be drained from them just to get my vision back.

"Why are you doing this?" I asked him.

He shrugged and simply said, "Because I can."

BY T. STYLES

As the words exited his lips, he thickened even more. He was so large maybe this is why he felt it was okay to rape people. Because no one that endowed could find a suitable partner.

Before I knew it, he was on top of me again. When I would awaken this time, I would be in an alley naked.

In a bad part of town.

CHAPTER TWENTY-THREE

B ack at home, in my room, I lay in bed trying to heal. The man I thought worked in the government, was a liar. He had pulled the same trick on other women and had never been caught. I pray that changed because he was a killer.

Sheree did all she could to help but couldn't do more because she had to work and get money. Mariah had called several times too and I wondered if Sheree called her for support, but I'll never know because I refused to see her.

Too embarrassed with how I looked.

Still, my cousin cooked for me, helped me bathe, and even laid in bed with me on the nights she could when she didn't have a client.

Through it all...I missed Hazel.

I wondered if she was okay and even thought about stalking her callers since the phone plan was in my name but didn't want to violate her trust even more. She had chosen to leave me out of her life.

So I would try to honor her request.

After what that man did to me, I needed 15 stitches in my face, and my shoulder was virtually dislocated from when he tied my wrist so tightly that it popped out of socket.

I was embarrassed, hurt, and more than anything…afraid.

Any noise, and I do mean any noise in the house sent me to the window checking for him. Wondering if he came back to finish me off.

One night it was so bad my cousin had to get real with me. "Maybe you shouldn't do this no more," Sheree said, looking at me as we both lay on my bed. "That shit fucked me up trying to find out where you were, only to see that he did this."

I nodded as tears ran down my face. "Please don't blame yourself," I said gently. "If anything I blame myself."

Just then, my phone rang.

Usually, it would be clients trying to hook up, but this time, when I looked at the screen, I saw a number I hadn't expected to see.

Giant.

"I have to take this," I told her, without saying who was on the line. Although I was done with him, I knew he had a hold of Hazel. So my main reason was trying to find out where she was.

She kissed my cheek, got out of bed, and closed the door behind her.

"Hello?"

"Damn, baby. What's wrong?" He asked.

I must have sounded like I was in pain. The real tea was I was so emotionally beaten, that just him asking immediately sent me to crying. Don't get it fucked up. I knew what kind of man he was...but still.

Even beaten dogs favor their owners sometimes.

Hoping to break down walls before I asked about Hazel, I told him about my devastating ordeal in Atlanta and how I was scared to sleep most nights.

"See, this my fault," he said. "I could've dealt with the nigga expeditiously."

He's right.

"I'll be fine."

"I should've never allowed you to get into this."

"You could never have stopped me from getting my money," I told him, finding myself needing to console him instead of the other way around. "So don't say that."

"It is my fault, Lisa," he insisted.

"Lisa?" Did he just call me another woman's name? I didn't care but still.

"I didn't say Lisa."

BY T. STYLES

He did. And he was lying too.

"Anyway, I thought we could do this together. Had I known we wouldn't, I would've never introduced you to this lifestyle. You could've been killed."

Okay he was having a Tyler Perry theater moment with all this overacting shit. And I wanted it to end.

"Where you at?" He asked.

"Home."

He sighed deeply. "Listen…I want you to meet me. Let's get something to eat."

"I look terrible," I told him.

"I don't care how you look. I just want you here with me. Can we at least pretend we still friends?"

It was just as I thought…everyone was looking at my condition. Because at the end of the day no matter how much makeup I put on my tattooed bruised face, you could still see I had been sent through the ringer.

Luckily, the expressions on their faces showed concern, not judgment.

I had stitches.

Bruises.

A dislocated shoulder.

I looked hideous.

But Giant seemed more worried about me than anything else. Damn he was good at this pimping shit. "I wanna talk to you about something," he said over his meal.

I nodded. This was what I wanted to get to.

Hazel.

"I want you to stay with me."

"What you mean stay with you?"

"At my house until you heal. It's the least I can do." He sighed. "Let me take care of you, Lemon."

My name was Jaystar, and him calling me my hoe name meant he still thought of me the same. This was a trap, but I would go into it for my friend.

"You really want me at your house?"

"Yeah, man," he said. "And I'm not talking about a motel either. I'm talking about really staying with me. As my girl."

"In that house?"

"Why you keep asking me that?"

My heart pounded in my chest. I didn't want to stay with this nigga. I wanted my friend. But I felt like this was a part of his game. "Do you have Hazel working for you?"

"I'm talking about you and you talking about a child?"

"I need to know what's going on. I saw you texted her one night."

Silence.

"Giant, if we gonna be real then—."

"Let's just say I have her where I want her." He sipped his drink. "Luckily I want you more. But you gotta cut all this extra shit out. I got clients that miss you, almost as much as I miss you too. So how you play your next move will determine what I do next."

He didn't know it, but I already wanted him dead. "So you want me to work for you? That's what you saying."

"Not at first. At least stay with me for a couple of months. Let me help you heal and get paid too. And then...if you don't wanna be with me, I'll let you go and Hazel too."

I ended up staying with him for about a week.

And every day I would ask about Hazel, and he would say…not yet.

It drove me insane, but I didn't let him know.

Luckily things were better than they had ever been between us. He waited for me to heal and when we were together we would spend our days doing little things around the massive home.

He even had the vaulted ceilings I always wanted. It was just…perfection.

But at night we stayed in the basement, which was cool but not as well taken care of as upstairs. I didn't get why we were there. And whenever I asked him he would tell me it's cooler down there.

Yeah aight.

There were two bedrooms in the basement, and it was almost as if he was hiding me. It even had its own entrance and exit.

Every other day I would ask about Hazel…and again he gave me nothing. Next to Sheree calling me like I was crazy and me avoiding her calls, knowing she would never want me to sell pussy again after what happened to me, I was growing impatient. If I brought back Hazel at least she would believe it wasn't in vain.

One night I woke up to him yelling. "Get up, Lemon! Now!"

Grabbing my robe, I walked up the steps and approached him. "What's wrong?"

"Somebody emptied my bank account," he said. "Took everything from me." Then he looked at me with a narrowed glare. "Was it you?"

Half sleep I said, "Me?" I placed a hand on my chest. "You sound crazy!"

He shook his head, like he was waking up from a bad dream. Then he grabbed me and pulled me into a hug. "I'm sorry, baby...but with everything going on, I can't even pay my mortgage." He flopped down onto the couch. "I'm officially on my dick."

I sat at his feet and laid my head on his knee. "I'm sorry, Giant." From the reflection on his watch I saw that he was glaring at me, although I wouldn't let him know.

He hated my guts. I could feel it.

"If I can't make this money back, I don't know what I may have to do. Most of the clients I have now like it young and I don't wanna do that. I would rather connect them with someone more experienced."

It was just like I thought. He was about to blackmail me with Hazel. And I knew what I had to do.

"Maybe I could go harder," I offered. "I'm not young but I can fake young in the bedroom."

From his watch I saw his sinister smile clearly. "I guess you'll have to do."

BY T. STYLES

CHAPTER TWENTY-FOUR

I sat in my car with the engine idling low, my fingers trembling over the call screen. Hazel's name was lit up again. For the sixth time. Maybe the seventh. I'd lost count on how many times I hit her.

Maybe I was obsessing too much.

It didn't matter because there was no answer.

Not a text. Not a "leave me alone." Just…silence.

So I did something I didn't want to do. I went through her call logs. Nothing. She wasn't even using the phone.

I stared out the windshield, the sky overcast and gray like it had been crying longer than me. My stomach twisted with guilt and something I couldn't name. Possibly regret. Possibly fear. I had made a deal with the devil, agreed to suck dicks for Giant, just to keep Hazel safe and she wasn't even talking to me.

And yet he refused to tell me where she was. Because one thing was for certain, I had paid someone to ask her mother straight up if she was at least living with her. And she told this person Hazel had not been home.

So why couldn't I find her?

I threw the car into drive and did the only thing that made sense...I headed back toward our old neighborhood. Every turn felt like driving deeper into a memory I didn't want to relive. Because I started to think about my mother.

My chest got tight as I pulled onto our old block, past the same corner store with the flickering sign, the same sidewalk cracks I used to skip over like it was a game.

Where was this girl?

On every block I tapped, I rolled down the window and asked anyone in earshot. First the older woman who always sold incense on the corner...no, she hadn't seen Hazel. Then two YN's sitting on bikes...they just shook their heads while one mouthed, "Get the fuck up out of here." Then there was a man sweeping outside the corner store who said he might've seen her "sometime last week," but he could be more accurate if I gave him some paper.

So it was fuck him for real.

In the end no one helped, and I was falling deeper and deeper into darkness.

Then I spotted her.

Leslie.

Hazel's friend...the same girl who gave me space to talk to Hazel the last day I saw her. She was walking down the sidewalk with her headphones half on and I pulled up on her smooth before parking and getting out.

"Hey!" I called, walking toward her.

She turned, eyes widening just a little when she saw me.

"I don't mean to bother you," I said, "but have you seen Hazel?"

She looked down at her sneakers. Her silence told me enough before she even opened her mouth. "I...I think..." she started, hesitating. "I think she's in the streets."

My stomach dropped. "What you mean in the streets?"

She sighed. "At first she was doing okay. Looked like things were working out. New clothes. Hair done. Nails. Shit like that...but lately..."

She was a slow talker which was annoying as fuck. "Lately what?" I asked, voice sharp. "What lately?"

"She don't look good," she said, eyes soft with something like pity. "Not like before when you took care of her. She was happy. And bragging about how much you loved her."

Was I supposed to be in so much pain hearing those words?

"But you can tell...I mean you can tell now the streets got her."

I nodded slowly, like my body was moving separate from my heart. "Thank you for being real with me. And whatever you do, don't tell her I been asking around, okay?"

The girl frowned, confused. "Why not?"

"Because I don't want *him* to know."

Before she could respond, I turned away and walked up the cracked steps toward my old apartment building.

The moment I crossed the threshold, it hit me.

That smell.

The combination of mold, grease, burnt hair, and bad memories. The walls were still the same stained yellow, the floors scuffed from years of lost battles. I looked over at the door where I once lived with my mother and rapist, the man who stole everything from me and took a deep breath.

I had to get out of here or I would suffer what Mariah said were panic attacks.

So I turned to my right.

Hazel's door.

And knocked.

172 **BY T. STYLES**

It shocked me when it creaked open with the lightest touch. On God my heart hit the floor. "Hazel?" I called, voice echoing too loud in the silent hallway.

No answer.

I stepped inside, slow and cautious. Basically nosey as fuck.

The apartment was stripped bare. Walls empty. Carpet stained. The kind of silence that didn't just feel quiet...but for some reason it felt wrong.

Did they...did she...move?

If so where was Hazel?

I stood in the middle of the room, spinning slowly in place, hoping for something...anything...that would give me a clue. But after what felt like forever I soon found that there was nothing.

CHAPTER TWENTY-FIVE

This client massaged my feet so long I dozed off.

Unlike the other times…when he'd tell me it was okay to catch a few z's, this time he seemed irritated when I woke up. "Sorry about that," I said.

He got up without a word, clicked on his watch, and stuffed his wallet into his pocket. That was his leaving ritual. "I know you don't expect me to pay for that," he said under his breath.

"Uh…yeah, I do. You asked to rub my feet, and I let you."

"But the part that works for me is when I'm pleasing you. Can't please you if you asleep."

Nigga you can't please me even if I wasn't.

This your kink not mine.

He was tripping. I was stacking and wasn't about to play with this nigga. "I need my money, so yeah, I do expect you to pay for it and be professional."

Then it hit me.

Back when Giant took advantage of me, at least he'd made sure the tricks paid. But now? I wasn't set up for digital payments yet. I'd either walk out broke or walk out wiser because those were my only two options.

So, remembering my plan, I sat on the edge of the bed, slid my feet into my shoes. "You don't wanna pay me? Fine. But you cut." I grabbed my purse, marched to the door.

My hand was on the knob when he said, "Here." I turned. He held out all my cash...plus a $20 tip. "Just fucking with you. I guess I miss you, that's all."

I smiled like it didn't sting. "Then the fuck you better act like it."

I was cruising down the street when I got a call. Nervous and excited, I quickly answered.

Hazel? I thought, hope already blooming too fast in my chest. But it wasn't her. It was the woman who gave me life. "Ma?"

Her voice crackled on the other end. It was thin. Shaky. Like it had been run through tears and then dried out by exhaustion. "Hey baby," she sniffled. "It's me."

Something in her tone made my stomach twist. "What's wrong?"

I hated how fast my voice turned soft. I hated how, even after everything, my first instinct was to give a fuck. But it was my mother, at one point my friend, and no matter how badly she'd hurt me, my heart still remembered how to worry.

"It's Marco," she whispered.

The name alone punched a cold hole in my chest. "What about him?"

"We fought," she said.

I sat there, stunned for only a second before I replied flatly, "Y'all always fight."

"This time was different, Babygirl," she said quickly. "It got bad. Real bad. So bad I was arrested last night."

That shut me up.

Not because she had never been arrested before. But because something in her voice sounded...empty. Like she had nothing left to throw. At the same time I couldn't give in too easily. "So what? You calling for bail money?"

Even as I said it, I hated myself. Still, when I was down, when I was crying in bathrooms and breaking silently, she didn't comfort me. So, why should I be there for her now?

"No, Babygirl. I bailed myself out," she said. "But now he's pressing charges."

176 **BY T. STYLES**

I swallowed hard, my hand tightening on the steering wheel. "So, what you want with me?"

"Actually…I need your help."

I didn't like how that sounded. "What that mean?"

She took a deep breath. "He said if you talk to him…tell him why you treated him badly when we all lived together, then maybe he'll drop the charges."

I blinked. My whole body froze like my blood had turned to ice. "And why would I do that?"

"Because he was like a father to you!"

"What?"

"He says he just wants to talk," she said, her voice rising. "It's not like that anymore."

So she did know what he did to me. "You asking me to talk to the man who terrorized me?" My voice was calm, but underneath it, rage was shaking me. At the end of the day I had yet to utter the words that he had been raping me since I was twelve.

"I'm asking you to help your mother," she snapped, instantly defensive. "Because I'm at a low point, Jaystar. I could go to jail for a long time."

I had to pull over because she sounded crazy. "Ma, you wouldn't even talk to me when I came to your job," I reminded her, my voice cracking despite myself. "Threw my flowers in the trash and everything."

"I ain't say nothing at first but now you calling me ma? Instead of mommy."

"Be glad I'm calling you that."

"You know what, this why I didn't want to call."

"Maybe you shouldn't have. Because right now, the only thing on my mind is Hazel. Not the way you ignored me when I brought you roses to your job."

"There you go bringing up old shit," she snapped again, sharper this time. "This why I don't like calling you. You always make it about the past. Trying to sound like I'm a bad mother."

"It's always about you," I shot back, louder.

Silence.

"Are you going to help me or not?" She said, flat. No emotion. "I'm saying..." she paused, "if you don't talk to him, like he asked, then I could go to jail."

So basically he wanted some pussy again.

I pressed my palm to my forehead, a hot sting behind my eyes. "Does he want to talk, or does he want...something else?"

"Jaystar, don't start."

"No, you don't start. Are you saying I should fuck him?"

"I would never tell my daughter to do something like that."

"Then what would you tell her to do?"

Silence.

"I'm saying…" her voice broke, barely above a whisper now, "if you don't help me, I could be locked up for a long time."

I exhaled hard. "What exactly did you do to him?"

"I stabbed him."

CHAPTER TWENTY-SIX

Inside of the basement of his house, I handed Giant the cash he said he needed for mortgage without making eye contact. Luckily with the hustle I had done I still had about five thousand on the ready, so I wasn't totally depleted.

My fingers brushed his for only a second, and I hated that he smiled at the touch like I had given him something sacred, maybe bits and pieces of myself.

"You got your money. Now where is she? And don't tell me she at the house because I know Ava moved."

His eyes flicked up lazily, as if I had interrupted a daydream. "Who we talking about again?" He asked, even though he knew damn well who I was talking about.

"Hazel," I said, trying to keep my voice even. "She's not answering her phone, and I know you know something."

He leaned back against the wall in his house, thick gold chain catching the dull light. "Haven't seen her," he repeated slowly. "Anyway she's not my responsibility. Or yours either."

"Giant...where is the girl?"

I watched him. Waited.

Then came a lazy grin that always told the truth better than his mouth ever could. "You got more?"

"More what?"

"Money." The words landed like a slap. No clarification. No attempt to clean it up.

Just you got more.

And I knew right then he wasn't going to tell me a damn thing unless I fed him his fee. Whatever that meant. "Stop the fucking games. You don't have to fake make me your girl no more. I turned twenty yesterday and don't need the lies anyway. What's your fee to let me get Hazel back?"

"Twenty thousand."

I clenched my jaw and looked down at my hands. My nails were still perfect. My polish unchipped. It was a stupid detail, but in that moment, it reminded me how well I played my role, even when everything inside me was breaking. "I'll be in touch."

He nodded, pocketing the money I had already given him. "Cool...just remember that yesterday's prices ain't tomorrow's price. So you better move quick."

I sat in the parking lot of the precinct for a long time. Watching people go in and out with troubles of their own. Mothers with crying kids. A man with a busted lip being guided in by his girlfriend. A teenage boy in cuffs, looking down at his shoes like he wanted to disappear.

And here I was, about to walk inside and do something I knew my neighborhood would never forgive me for.

Snitch.

The word echoed in my chest like a siren. You weren't supposed to talk to police. Not even if you were the one hurting. But Hazel was missing. And the only man who might know something wasn't saying shit.

Bitch ass nigga.

Then he had the nerve to be upping the price so he could squeeze everything out of me I had left, plus a few bills more. When I knew he didn't need me. Something else was up and I didn't know what.

Anyway, I was done talking.

Instead, I walked into the doors.

BY T. STYLES

Inside the station was too cold, too bright, and smelled like overbleached floors and burnt coffee. My palms were slick with sweat and my knees trembled. Still I stood tall as I approached the front desk.

I don't give a fuck if I was a hoe or not.

I had rights too.

The officer behind the glass barely glanced up. "Can I help you?"

"I need to talk to someone," I said, trying to keep my voice steady. "About a missing girl."

He finally looked at me, tired eyes lifting just slightly. "You file a report?"

"I don't want to file. I just—" I inhaled. "What can I do if I think my boyfriend is involved in a young girl's disappearance? Possibly even being trafficked."

That got his attention. "Trafficked how?"

Was there more than one way?

I looked down at my hands. I hadn't rehearsed this part.

"He was texting her," I said quietly. "She was staying with me...but...um not anymore. The important thing to realize though is that she's thirteen. And he started texting her...buying her new clothes and now she's gone."

He sat back, pen pausing over a pad. "Do you have the messages? That he texted her."

"Uh...no...but I saw his name on her phone the night before she disappeared."

"That's not proof."

"I know. I just...it's just that I know him. And she wouldn't just run off like that without saying something to me."

"Where is her mother? Or father."

Fuck...with every question I was being pushed further back from getting some help. Ava didn't care about her daughter. I was it for Hazel.

"They aren't involved."

"So who has custody?"

"Me...I mean her mother...but it's complicated."

He gave me that look...the one that said he's already decided. "Unless you have physical evidence, messages, or witnesses, there's not much we can do. Maybe she's with family?"

"Nah...she was living with me," I said, heat rising in my face. "Because her mother's a pill head and nobody else gives a fuck."

"That's just like so what."

"Excuse me?"

He leaned forward, tone softening, like pity made up for the uselessness. "If anything turns up, come back. But I'm gonna be honest. We'll need proof. Real proof."

"Short of catching him in action what kind?"

"Like I said...until then, keep trying to reach her. We'll keep it on record." The man didn't even bother to ask their names.

I nodded stiffly, already backing away. Not because I was done...but because I knew when a system wasn't built for girls like Hazel.

So I was gonna have to make them listen.

CHAPTER TWENTY-SEVEN

My next client was later that night. If I was gonna help Hazel, stack and activate a weak plan in my mind I had to get cleaned up and ready. But when I pulled up to the house, my cousin Sheree was outside, leaning against her car, breathing heavy. I had been dodging her since I started talking back to Giant, even though we were done now.

I knew she was mad.

"What's wrong with you?" I asked.

"Better question, is it true you working for Giant again?" She stood straight, eyes burning. "Because I thought we were partners."

"It's not like you think it is. Because he—"

"Then why people saying y'all partners?" She cut me off. "After everything he did to you—"

"What is your thing with him? Why you hate him so—."

"Because he shot me!" She yelled. "The bullet in my arm you love talking about, came from that nigga."

"Sheree, I...I didn't know."

"How could you? I warned you to stay away from him and you didn't listen."

BY T. STYLES

"Cuz, I'm soo—."

"I don't need your pity."

I could tell there was nothing I could say to make things better. So to get her out my face, for now at least, I decided to be mean. Because she hated when people had an attitude problem.

"I'm using him for my own reasons. So stay out my business."

I tried to sidestep her to get into the house and up to my room, but she grabbed my locs...hard. Pain shot through my scalp as she continued to tug to get me off balance. We'd never fought before, but there was no time to process. She meant harm.

"What the fuck you doing?"

"I can't believe you back with that nigga!" She yelled, yanking me closer. "Letting him drag you back into his bullshit! He's gonna get your ass killed!"

Was she really fighting me because of Giant? Like this can't be my life.

"The only one that's trying to get me killed is you."

I didn't want to hurt her like I knew I could. But it was hard considering her fists flew wild and free. In my mind beating her like I knew I could was not an option.

So I shoved her with everything I had and bolted for the house's door.

Locked.

Fuck!

She caught me, wrapped both arms around my waist, and slammed me to the ground like a wrestler. I kicked and flailed, but it was useless...this bitch rained down hits like I was a punching bag.

Finally, I went limp. Let her wear herself out. I think it was the guilt of getting Hazel wrapped in all this shit because I had given up. Maybe I deserved all of this. Mariah had told me that Hazel was watching me, wanting to be like me, and I ignored it all. Maybe I was getting exactly what I deserved.

Minutes later, tired like we went one on one, she stood over me, panting. "You got a week to get out and find someplace else to stay. After that, I want you gone."

My next client was a regular...the one Angry Angie swore paid well and treated me right. So when he found my secret account and we connected, I expected a little extra outside of the fee I usually demanded.

BY T. STYLES

Now inside of the room, after having made him moan, I watched him climb off me and act like he was headed for the door. "Excuse me! Where's my paper?"

"You don't look the same," he said. "Your body don't even smell the same. Like you not letting the rot off of one man get up off you before you fuck another."

"What did you just say?"

"You look a mess."

I shook my head, shrugged. "And what the fuck that got to do with you? You busted a nut the same as any other time."

"When I was paying you before, you had a certain look. Now?" He gestured at my bruises...arms, legs, face. "You show up battered and still expecting top pay?"

"I just fought my cousin. But I'm here. Pussy wet. And clean. Business is business." I leveled my stare. "So give me my money. Now!"

He rushed the bedside I guess preparing to hit me because his chest was heaving. I knew what this was. He wanted an excuse to hurt me. Wanted it bad. If I wasn't careful, he'd do worse than the serial killer ever had.

"You know what, keep it," I whispered. "But lose my number. And I'ma put the word out to other women too. You gonna be short out here. So you better start cruising the streets."

"That's fine with me." He laughed softly before settling down. "Maybe you should've kept your nigga around."

"The thing you forgot is this...there's a reason why I knew so much about you. Why I requested to see your license and socials. Because if you think this gonna slide with no kickback...let's just say..." I laughed to myself as I slid off the bed. "You know what, never mind."

He smirked, grabbed his wallet, burrowed inside and tossed the cash onto the bed. "You better get back up with Giant. At least he can protect you. Because if you ever threaten me again you dead."

"There won't be an again with us, nigga."

"You got that right."

The door slammed behind him after he walked out.

Fuck him.

I stood across the street from my old apartment, arms folded tight across my chest. I didn't bother going

190

BY T. STYLES

inside. Instead I stood on the porch and that's when I saw her. Hazel's other friend.

Shawny.

She was young, smart-mouthed, always had something slick to say. But her eyes changed when she saw me. Like she had pity on me.

"Hey," I said, voice lower than usual. "You got a second?"

She nodded. "Let's go inside the building."

I didn't want to, but I followed her. She leaned on the wall, closest to the mailboxes. "You look tired."

"I am." I took a breath. "And I need your help."

She blinked. "Hazel again? 'Cause people been talking about how you won't leave that girl alone. What you some type of dyke?"

"Fuck you say to me?"

"I'm just playing."

Ew, she was annoying. "Listen, I'm worried about her."

"Well I can't help you."

"I think you can." I pulled a folded twenty from my pocket and pressed it into her hand. "I'll give you more if you help. Just...talk to people. Listen to what they saying and tell me when I come back."

She looked down at the money. Nodded and took it from my hand. "Alright. I'll ask around. But I will say this...I don't do short money. Next time make it a hundred minimum." She walked out popping gum.

These new kids different.

When I came back the next day she had a little more information. "I can't do nothing else for you."

I frowned. "Why not?"

"Because somebody came up to me earlier today. Told me to stop asking questions about her...or else."

She gave me the twenty back.

BY T. STYLES

CHAPTER TWENTY-EIGHT

I was exhausted when I pulled up to the house…my body moving on autopilot. When I walked toward my room as I turned the corner, my stomach lurked…my door stood wide open. When I stepped inside, what I saw made my knees weak. Giant was sitting on the edge of my bed, watching me.

I shook my head. "What you doing here?"

"I need more money."

"I'm not giving you shit. You not helping me…so why should I help you?" I leaned against the wall, staring at the ceiling.

"You really went to the police?"

My heart dropped. "I don't know what you—."

"No need in lying." He moved closer. "Unless you get me another $5,000, you won't see that little bitch again, because trust me I can make more than that off her."

"I promise if you hurt her I'll—."

"You not doing shit. Plus the fee is for you breaking code." He walked up to me and grabbed my arm. "And if you ever go to the cops again, I'll snap her neck. And then snap yours."

His cologne still hung in the air...sweet and bitter. A smell that used to make me feel safe now twisted my stomach. I stared at the spot on my sheets he sat on, like it might give me some kind of explanation.

I dropped my keys on the dresser harder than I meant to, spun around, and went straight for the kitchen. Sheree was standing by the sink, scrolling her phone like nothing happened. Like she hadn't just let the one man I was trying to escape sit in the same space where I slept.

"You let him in my fucking room?" I asked, barely above a whisper.

She looked up slowly, eyebrows raised like I was bothering her. "Your room?" She repeated. "Let's get something straight. This my house. You rented a space for which you got five days left. And what are you even talking about anyway?"

"You playing with my life with that nigga."

She shook her head and dragged a hand down her face. Then she took a deep breath. "You back with him anyway. So what difference does it make?"

"I'm not back with him," I snapped. "So why the fuck you let him in?"

And then it dawned on me. I could tell in her eyes that she had no idea he was in her house. So how was he able to get past her? "You didn't know did you?"

"Just leave me alone, Jay."

I wanted to scream. To shake her. To tell her everything. That I was only dealing with Giant to protect Hazel. That I'd put myself back in harm's way just to keep that little girl from drowning in the same mess I'd been born into.

But I couldn't.

Because right now, I didn't trust her.

"Whether you did or didn't, I'm still paying rent. Actually I'm paid up for at least eight months. So don't ever let anybody back in my room again."

CHAPTER TWENTY-NINE

*L*emon didn't knock, she banged on Angie's door.

Because she wanted answers on who Giant really was, and she knew just who to get them from. Although she normally met her at the motel, this time would be different.

Angry Angie lived in a brick row home with paint peeling from the banister and wind chimes that sounded more like screams than bells.

When the door finally cracked open, Angie's sharp brown eyes peered through the space. "Lemon." Her tone was flat. Suspicious. "Fuck you doing here? And why you banging on my door like that?"

"I need to talk to you," Lemon said, her voice tight with exhaustion. "About Hazel."

At first, Angie didn't move. But something in Lemon's face...maybe the serious look behind her eyes, shifted something in her soul. So she opened the door all the way and motioned inside.

Lemon was shocked because despite its exterior the house was cozy. She could also tell she came at dinner time because along with incense she smelled fried food.

BY T. STYLES

Walking deeper, she followed Angie to the small kitchen, where a chipped glass ashtray overflowed, and a half-drunk bottle of Hennessey sat next to an open Bible.

"Why you asking me about your child?"

"She's not my child. She's my friend."

"Well I don't get involved in Giant's business no more," Angie said, lighting a cigarette with a trembling hand. "You know how it goes."

That was new news.

"Why?"

"What do you want, girl? The next thing I say will be get the fuck out on the way to the door."

She took a deep breath. "He won't tell me where Hazel is. She's been gone for days."

Angie's brows lifted, but her mouth stayed closed. She lit a cigarette and pulled. "What that got to do with me? Every hoe I know started selling pussy young."

Angie called herself being nasty, but Lemon picked up on the pain behind her tone. "She's not that kind of kid, Angie," Lemon added, her voice cracking. "She trusted me. I was the only one she had. Maybe if someone fought for me...and you..." She touched her arm before pulling her fingers back slowly. "Maybe we wouldn't have had to stay in for so long." She paused. "She's only thirteen."

At that, something in Angie shattered.

She leaned back, eyes distant. "Thirteen," she breathed out. "Same age as my baby girl."

Silence.

Lemon walked closer, afraid she would destroy the bridge she felt was being laid.

"He did the same thing to my daughter when she was that age," she finally said. "She over twenty now but the past is still crystal. He bought her fancy clothes. Took her and her little friends out to eat. Gave 'em spending money. Made her feel like a princess...like she was special. You tell me how a mother's love can compete with that?"

"I would have chosen you over him," Lemon said with her entire heart. "A thousand times. I don't care what he bought me."

Angie weakened in that moment even more.

"How was he able to get to her?"

"Kept me busy. Said he had a babysitter. I believed him. Plus he was a friend. I was close to his ex-girlfriend Lisa."

Lemon frowned because she remembered the name. He called her that by mistake not too long back.

"Next thing I know, she ain't coming home for days. And when she did... she looked like somebody I ain't birth."

Lemon felt her chest tighten.

"I tried to stop it," Angie continued, eyes growing glassy. "But by then, it was too late. Now she talks to me like I'm just

198   BY T. STYLES

some lady who helped start her career. It's all business...no love. Ain't no mother-daughter left. Just pain in its place. With Giant as her sponsor."

"Then you know what he's doing to Hazel," Lemon whispered. "You know it. If you couldn't help your little girl, help Hazel." Lemon took a deep breath and looked down. "Help me."

Angie suddenly started pacing. "I can't go to the cops. I just can't. Too much history and don't nothing change history except more."

"So you tried with your daughter, and they did nothing."

Her cold stare told Lemon she had.

"I need you, Angie."

She stopped in front of Lemon. "You don't know what he has on me. The stuff I done, the names I done gave him."

"Then give me something. Anything. A direction. A clue."

Angie shook her head, but her lips trembled. "I already gave you the biggest clue I got. He grooms 'em early. Real early. Before they even know they're being groomed. And he puts them on display at those parties." She sighed. "In his mind they dollars, in their hearts he's love."

I thought about my ex-boyfriend Smack. He was forty-two years old when we started dating. He did the same to me when I was thirteen and I thought it was love too.

"You know something else, Angie. Please." Lemon felt like the floor shifted under her. Her fists clenched so tight her knuckles whitened. "Angie," she begged, "please help us."

But Angie was already sitting back down, turning away. "I'm sorry, baby. I can't."

Lemon didn't move for a long moment. Besides it was the first time she didn't call her out her name.

Instead, she stared at the woman who, in another life, might've been an ally. A savior. But in this world, Angie was just another survivor. And survivors rarely speak because some never know what it means to be safe.

BY T. STYLES

CHAPTER THIRTY

I just walked out of Angie's house when my phone rang.

There I was, staring at the rusted gate like it had answers buried in the metal. The sky was turning orange, that kind of soft dusk that should've felt peaceful but to me it was all heavy.

My cousin Sheree wasn't talking to me.

Giant had Hazel.

And I had zero answers.

So when my phone rang and I saw Mommy on the screen, I wanted to toss it in the gutter.

But I didn't.

I picked up, bracing myself for the worst because lately that's all it had been. "You think you can come by the house and talk to Marco?"

No *Hello*. No *How are you*.

Just that voice, that question, thick with expectation.

My stomach twisted, and my grip on the phone tightened. "Like I told you before, why would I do that?"

"You know why. So he'll drop the charges."

Was this real life? I don't know if separating from her so long had me seeing things differently, but I was angry. Here it was I just left a woman who wanted a connection with her daughter while mine…never mind.

"You really asking me to talk to that man?" I snapped, louder than I meant to. "The same man who —"

"I know what he did," she cut in, her voice quick and sharp. But then it cracked, and suddenly she was crying. Real, messy crying. "It's just that I can't go to jail, Jaystar. I can't. I got no one but you."

I leaned against a brick wall, closing my eyes so tight it hurt. My chest burned from holding everything in. All the times I wanted to talk to her about life when I was younger, even about my relationship with Smack who I obviously never should've been with, and she gave me nothing. It was becoming crystal that she didn't give a fuck.

But she was my mother.

And I was tired.

"Where is he?" I whispered.

"At the house."

With me relenting, suddenly she sounded as right as rain.

Isn't that something?

Lemon climbed the cracked concrete steps of her old apartment building slowly, her heart thudding in her chest like it remembered every beat of pain stored in the walls.

When she reached the floor, she turned right out of instinct. Her feet carried her to the door that once belonged to Hazel, and she raised her hand. Preparing to knock, she caught herself.

She pushed the door open instead...

Why was the door still open?

Curious, she looked inside. The place was still empty, bare floors, stripped curtains, nothing left but dust and echoes. Letting out a long, tight breath, she turned left, where her mother lived. The door, just as her mother said, wasn't locked.

Lemon hesitated, then slowly twisted the knob and stepped inside.

There he was.

On the same sunken couch where so many of her memories had died, looking the fuck terrible. Where her childhood was smothered and replaced with silence. His eyes met hers, casual and cruelly calm.

"Why you here?" He asked.

Lemon closed the door behind herself and locked it with a firm click. She stayed there, back pressed to the wood like it was the only thing holding her upright. "I'm here because I don't want you to press charges on my mother."

Marco chuckled and tilted his head. "Why shouldn't I? She stabbed me." He raised his dingy white t-shirt to show the four stitches on his belly before dropping it again.

Lemon smiled. She liked him bruised, knicked and stabbed.

"That might be true," she said, keeping her voice as steady as she could. "But she's sorry. Plus she's your woman and it's her first charge."

He patted the space next to him on the couch. "Come sit."

Lemon didn't move.

"That wasn't a request," he replied.

Her fingers clutched into fists. Slowly, like her body was moving through mud, she stepped forward and sat at the edge of the cushion...just close enough to satisfy him.

"You're still beautiful," Marco said, reaching out to finger one of her yellow locs, his touch slow and unwelcome. "I see life been treating you good. It's in your eyes."

She flinched but held her ground. "Are you gonna drop the charges?" She asked, pushing the words past the lump in her throat. "Because I'm here like you requested."

"Only if you agree to your part in all of it."

Her brows drew together. "What part?"

"Your mother said you came here to make things better," he said, eyes gleaming. "To pay the debt."

"So you did know I was coming? Even though you asked what I was doing here." Lemon stared at him. "And what do you want with me?"

"Don't play dumb," he said, his voice dropping low. "You and I both know what I been missing."

The truth hit her like a blow. Her mother had sold her. Again. Like a trade to erase her own mistake.

Lemon rose.

"Where you going?" Marco asked, sounding amused.

She didn't look at him. Her body was steady…strength under the grief. Without another word, she walked to the door, unlocked it with trembling hands, and opened it wide.

"You'll be back," he announced. "Trust me."

Suddenly curiosity got her for a moment. "Why did she stab you?"

"Because when we were together, I called out your name."

CHAPTER THIRTY-ONE

*T*he street leading to Mariah's building was quiet, but the storm inside Lemon couldn't be silenced.

Tears clung to her lashes and spilled down her cheeks as she walked, her steps slow and unsteady. Her breath came in short bursts, chest heaving beneath her jacket, the betrayal from her mother still an open fucking wound.

She didn't even know why she ended up at her friend's house. It was probably the need to connect with the one person who gave her safety.

Her best friend Mariah.

When she reached the familiar door, she didn't knock hard. Just one soft tap.

Mariah opened the door as if she'd been expecting her all along. A real friend since day one, she didn't ask questions. She just stepped aside, letting Lemon in like she had a key.

The living room looked different now. The last time Lemon was there, there'd been folding chairs and a cold floor to sit on. Now, a soft gray sofa stretched along one wall, a small footstool sat nearby, and everything smelled like lavender and faint incense. Even the dog, the one who had once started a fire in the kitchen, was gone.

BY T. STYLES

"Nice sofa," Lemon whispered. It wasn't until then that she realized she hadn't seen or talked to her in months. Although you wouldn't know it by the way Mariah was acting, kind, welcoming, forgiving.

"Got it with the money you send me from time to time. Although I never knew why you was giving me money through my Cash Media account."

Silence.

"Well you might as well try it since you bought it," Mariah giggled softly, motioning to the couch. "Go on...get comfortable."

On her order, Lemon sank into the sofa, letting her body melt into the cushion as if it were a warm hug. Her legs trembled beneath her, but Mariah gently lifted them and placed them on the footstool, then draped a red knit blanket across her lap.

Nothing else was said.

The silence felt like love.

Lemon didn't know how long she cried, her shoulders shaking, her body folding in on itself, but she noticed the smell of something warm and earthy rising from the kitchen.

Mariah's tea.

Normally she'd refuse but she'd kill for a cup now.

When she returned, she handed Lemon a mug that was warm to the touch, steam rolling upward like a whisper. The scent was familiar…chamomile, mint…and the calming undertone of cannabis.

Mariah sat next to her, thigh to thigh, her presence steady. Only then did she speak. "You don't have to talk if you don't wanna."

Lemon opened her mouth, but the pain surged up too fast. "My mother… she – " Her voice cracked and collapsed. "You were right about her. She…she never gave a fuck about…"

"I wish I wasn't," Mariah said, not needing her to finish the sentence.

"I'm so grateful for you."

Mariah breathed deeply and then exhaled long. "God gives everybody a set of real-life guardian angels. We might be high, broke or don't know what to say sometimes but we be perfect for the right person. And in this life, I'm yours and you mine. And if your mother too stupid to get how special…"

Lemon shook her head no. "I'm nobody. I'm not special!"

Mariah firmly raised her chin. "If she don't get how fucking special my friend is, then fuck her with the diseasest dick I can find!"

For the first time Lemon laughed as Mariah rubbed her back gently, not pushing her to much else. The soft circles of her palm on Lemon's spine were grounding.

"You're a great person and a loving woman. Don't let your mother's stupidity break you."

208 **BY T. STYLES**

Silence and a sip of tea.

"I can't find Hazel," Lemon added, voice lower now. "I think... I think Giant sold her. And it's my fault."

Mariah turned to her, voice firm but full of care. "After all this time don't you get it? You not trying to save Hazel. You trying to save yourself."

Lemon sighed.

"And you can't do that until you stop running. Until you give your mother and Marco the full weight of what they deserve. You need to free yourself from them. For real this time."

"Okay, let's say I am trying to save myself, will you help me?"

"I been waiting forever to hear you say those words. 'Cause if finding that little girl means my best friend is finally free, sign me up."

Lemon stared at her, tears flooding her eyes again, too full of everything to respond. Her hands trembled as she clutched the mug. Placing the cup down, she turned toward Mariah and collapsed into her arms.

"I'm gonna come up with a plan."

Mariah nodded sinisterly. "You just make sure you let me in on it."

CHAPTER THIRTY-TWO

I had just pulled away from Mariah's place, the taste of her tea still warm in my mouth, when my phone buzzed. I saw my mother's name light up the screen, and for the first time in forever, I didn't answer.

So I planned to let it go to voicemail, convincing myself it was the right thing. That I didn't owe her my attention. But then…curiosity got the better of me.

So I answered.

And her voice hit like a slap to my heart.

"I can't believe I trusted your fucking ass," she spat, each word sharp as shattered glass.

"Mommy?" She had never cut me like that before, so I had to make sure it was her.

"You so stupid and fucking selfish. I asked you for one fucking thing, and you can't even do that shit!"

Silence.

"All you had to do was talk to him and say sorry for disrespecting him the last time you were there with your little friend. I mean are you that fucking disobedient that you can't do what I'm asking?"

Yep, it was definitely my mother.

BY T. STYLES

Finally it was my time to speak. "I will never forget this call. And trust me, you will live to regret it."

By the time it ended, I didn't even realize I had stopped breathing until I exhaled.

My vision blurred. My hands slipped off the wheel. I swerved just enough to make my heart jerk, and I had to pull over before I ended up hurting myself or somebody else.

The engine purred quietly as I sat on the shoulder of the road, surrounded by night.

I should've expected it.

Wanting to reclaim my heart, I rested my head on the steering wheel. My fingers gripped it tight, my knuckles pale under the pressure. "Get it together," I whispered to myself.

I sat back, took a shaky breath, and turned the car key halfway to listen to the engine breathe without moving. I didn't know what was going to happen next, but I was done being scared.

It was time to choose violence with these niggas.

I pulled up to Giant's house.

Let's just say he wasn't expecting me.

I rounded the corner, ready to text him to come outside.

And then I saw *her* even though where I was parked, she couldn't see me. Driving deeper into the trees on the property, I parked and got out.

I had to get a better look.

A black town car pulled up, clean and quiet, and from it stepped a woman. She looked like she was a superstar's girlfriend and had a buss down with a middle part which was crispy black. The woman had to be twenty-six and she was tall and graceful, with skin that glowed and gold bracelets that caught the light from their property. Sleek like a panther, she wore a black trench coat and a red catsuit.

On God it looked like she had nothing to prove. I got the impression she was exactly who she thought she was.

When the trunk of the car popped open, a man handed her two matching suitcases.

Wait…did she…did she live here?

And did she know although briefly, I once did?

I stopped breathing.

BY T. STYLES

She walked right up to the front door. Not the side. Not the basement. Not with hesitation.

She used her own key.

I couldn't move, especially since Giant would usher my ass downstairs like the family pet.

Moments later the door shut behind her with a soft, final click.

I walked back to my car slowly, legs like water, and sank into my driver's seat. Confused, I pulled my knees up to my chest and wrapped my arms around them. In the shadows of this big house I remained, looking at the mansion I probably helped pay for and tried to figure out what part of my chest was hurting the most.

My throat? My ribs? My heart?

Something inside me was splitting open.

Not only did he tell me it was cooler to sleep in the basement, but he also told me the rooms in the house were under renovation.

Straight up his bitch ass lied.

Did she...could she know about me?

I stared at my phone, thumb hovering over his name. I couldn't bring myself to call. Not yet. I wanted answers, but not the kind that punch you in the gut.

When I saw a groundskeeper I had seen before walking down the pathway balancing a ladder on his shoulder and a toolbox in the other hand, I placed my feet down. I once gave him a meal after I saw him working all day. He was grateful and I'm hoping he'll give me a little gratitude now. He looked surprised when he saw me sitting in my car.

"Oh," he said. "Didn't see you there."

I blinked, my voice cracking before I even got the words out. "That woman who just went in the front door...who is she?"

He paused, shifting the weight of the ladder. "Giant's wife." The way he said it, I knew he wanted me to know. But more than anything, to get the fuck on with my life.

Everything inside me went still.

Wife.

Not girlfriend. Not business partner.

Wife.

I couldn't speak.

BY T. STYLES

CHAPTER THIRTY-THREE

Ever since I saw that woman walk through the front door with her key and her suitcases like she owned the place I'd been on a mission. Not because I wanted Giant. But the lies he put in place when I came to him as a woman looking for opportunity, only for him to switch it into something that sounded like he wanted a wife, was bizarre. I didn't cry.

I didn't scream.

I worked.

I took on more clients than I'd ever handled in my life. I said yes to people I used to dodge. People who talked too much, people who didn't tip, people who rubbed me the wrong way. Yes I should've walked away.

But when you're in hell you have to go through fire to get out.

So the danger didn't matter. Every dollar I earned felt like armor. Like power.

Every time Giant called, and he had zero info about Hazel, I told him the same thing.

"I'm with a client."

"I'm working."

"I'll call you later."

I started using words like "later" the way he used to use "soon."

He didn't like that, but unless he was telling me where baby girl was, which he wasn't, we weren't talking on his timeline. At the same time. I didn't push him too far away because I needed to make sure I found Hazel one day and he may be the aux in it all.

But for now it was truly, Fuck Giant. And his beautiful wife too.

CHAPTER THIRTY-FOUR

G iant stared at the phone in his hand, the call screen gone black. Lemon had hung up on him.

Hung up on him.

Did she have dementia? Did she forget the beatdown he gave her not too long ago?

The air in the bedroom thickened. His chest rose and fell, slower at first...then faster. Rage crawled up his throat like bile. He tossed the phone onto the bed beside him, where it bounced twice before landing on the comforter like a dare.

He lay there, motionless, his jaw clenched so tight the muscle twitched.

The disrespect twisted in his gut like wire.

He turned onto his side abruptly, fists balled in the sheets...then froze.

Then, a hand rested lightly on his shoulder.

Soft.

Familiar.

Possessive in its own way.

His wife.

She stirred beside him, still half-asleep, her breathing steady, unaware of the storm brewing inches away from her.

Although beautiful, she was also annoying.

Boring.

Consistent.

He swung his legs over the edge of the bed and stood up, his bare feet hitting the cool hardwood with a soft thud. Sassy as ever, he stormed toward the bathroom, the anger in him roiling like a storm tide.

But instead of going inside, he paused and reached for his phone again before scrolling. When he found what he was looking for, he pressed a name he had no right to press as it was given to him for emergencies only.

In the event something ever happened to Lemon while out on the street. It was her request not his.

The line rang twice.

Then:

Lemon's mother said, "Hello?"

"Debra, your daughter out here selling pussy." He came in ashy...wrong...mean. "I didn't wanna say nothin', but it's gotten outta hand now," he continued. "I thought you should know what kinda shit she be into."

Silence.

Then Debra's voice returned. Low. Controlled. Cutting. "Fuck you and that bitch too."

Click.

Giant's face burned with embarrassment, as he dog walked himself back to bed, and up under his wife's titties.

218

CHAPTER THIRTY-FIVE

I had just finished with a client.

The sun was sliding low in the sky, leaving gold smudges on the sidewalk as I climbed the steps to my room. My body ached in that way it always did after too many hours spent being everything for everyone...except myself.

I reached for my keys, my phone buzzing in my other hand. And when I glanced down I saw the number blinking on the screen.

On God I wished this bitch would leave me alone. Still I answered. "Hello?"

Her voice came through slow and uncertain. "How are you?"

Silence.

I stood in the doorway of my room, key still dangling from the lock, lips pressed tight. She made her choice.

So die in it for all I cared.

"What the fuck you want?" I finally asked.

Her voice cracked. "Wow."

"You don't get no more of my time. Now what the fuck you want with me?"

And then with fire she let me have it, "While you so busy talking to your mother like that...just know this...I heard you out there whoring yourself. Is that true?"

I laughed.

Cold.

Bitter.

I clenched the phone tighter. "If I am, it's better than giving it away to your nigga for free."

Silence.

"Well your boyfriend called and told me."

"Smack?"

"Nah...that other one with the Benz."

My blood boiled so fast I could barely speak. "I don't know what you talking about."

"Yes you do. The one who married to Shonda. The girl that owns all them braiding salons." She continued, obviously knowing more than me. "Now I don't know what you doing, but if what he told me is true, you better get it together. Especially considering the fact that I saw him with that little girl earlier today."

I was stuck. "What...what little girl?"

"The one that used to live next-door. Ava's daughter. And she looks way growner than twelve years old. That's for sure. Face painted up like a two-dollar hoe. Now let me see your smart mouthed ass handle that!"

The rage settled in my bones like thunder.

I didn't call Giant. I decided to show up. Not to the side door like some secret. But to the mothafucking front.

Once there I walked up the steps and turned the knob, praying it was unlocked.

It was.

And as angry as I was, that felt like all the permission I needed.

The door creaked open, and the inside of the house smelled like sandalwood and lies. I stepped deeper in, and barely two seconds later, I heard him scrambling around the corner, rushing in from the side, panic written across his face.

"What the...what the fuck you doing?" He barked, trying to block my path.

I stepped right past him. "I live here remember?"

"Bitch, don't play with me!"

"Why did you call my fucking mother?" I yelled.

He blinked. "Because you doing things you shouldn't be doing."

I laughed in his face. "The only thing we got to talk about is Hazel. Now where the fuck is she, Giant? She told me she was with you. Tell me the truth before I ruin your life. And before you think it's a game, understand that at this point I have nothing to lose."

"I'm not letting nobody fuck with my money. Even you."

I looked him square in the eyes.

I didn't flinch.

I stepped in closer, voice low and solid.

"Did you put her on the streets?"

He laughed. "Fuck you think."

"I want you to remember the day I gave you a chance."

Then I turned and walked out. Through the front door. Like I should have a long time ago.

CHAPTER THIRTY-SIX

*T*he car smelled like smoke and sweat; the windows cracked just enough to let the haze float out in lazy curls. The ashtray overflowed with half-smoked blunts, and a plastic cup of watered-down soda sat in the cupholder between them. Outside, a dingy motel blinked with a flickering neon "Vacancy" sign that buzzed like a mosquito in the silence.

They had been sitting there for over an hour and a half because Larron told him after following Lemon that he last saw her go there.

So as Larron shifted in the passenger seat, blowing out smoke and watching it disappear toward the windshield he said, "How long we gonna sit out this bitch?" Eyes still trained on the cracked window for the motel's front office.

Giant didn't look at him.

He leaned forward, his arm slung over the steering wheel, gaze locked on the row of rooms like a man waiting for something to break. "You know what...you talking way too fucking much for me."

Larron raised an eyebrow.

"I'm confused, man. You got a wife...a bad one at that. Big money. And we out here watchin' a – what? Motel hookup for one of your whores."

Giant turned his head slow, eyes sharp. "Don't ever forget my wife got there because I put her there...just like this whore upstairs she ain't shit without me." His voice came low and venom-laced.

Larron held up a hand. "Aight, damn."

Giant looked back at the motel. "And as for why we out here so long, it's because Lemon don't seem to understand that shit."

Larron leaned back, arms crossed. "My thing is this, I never seen you geek out over a female like this before. Not even your wife. Make it make sense."

Giant didn't answer.

He just stared harder at the row of rooms.

Annoyed.

Embarrassed.

Trapped in the very web he'd woven.

Instead of replying, he pulled out his phone and dialed a number he should never have. The police.

"911 what's the emergency?"

Larron sat up straighter. "Yo, what you – "

Giant waved him off. "Yeah, I wanna report some suspicious activity. At Motel East Ridge. It's room 208. I heard somebody screaming and I'm not sure what's going on."

Satisfied he hung up before they could ask further details.

Larron exhaled sharply. "That's grimy, nigga. Karma may come back and bite your ass."

"I don't believe in all that shit."

"Maybe that's the problem."

Ten minutes later, red and blue lights bloomed at the edge of the lot. From where their car sat, low, tucked between two SUVs, they had a perfect view of the action.

Two officers approached the door to Room 208 as Giant leaned forward, elbows on the dashboard as if he was watching a good movie.

But what happened next made him flinch. The door opened and Lemon stepped out wearing a pearl-colored silk robe, loose at the collar. She looped her arm around the waist of the white man standing next to her, tall, silver-haired, expensive watch gleaming even under the cheap lights.

Then she kissed him. Full on the lips. Like they went together.

She turned to the officers with a soft laugh and said something he couldn't hear. Whatever she said must've worked, because the cops nodded, gave an apologetic smile, and left without any more motion.

In the car, Giant's fist clenched around the steering wheel and his jaw twitched.

His friend turned slowly. "Yo...she played that shit smooth."

Giant didn't respond.

He couldn't. Besides, she had used his own teachings against him. The same tricks. The same strategies. The same confidence. And now, she was beating him at his own game.

As Lemon watched the squad cars pull away, her eyes flicked briefly toward the shadows where Giant's ride sat.

She saw him.

And smiled.

The late morning sun bounced off the cracked windows of Angry Angie's house, barely filtering through the thick smoke curling around her ceiling fan. Angie sat in her living room wearing a faded light blue robe, one leg tucked under the other, an ashtray on her lap already crowded with cigarette butts. The news was on low, something about a city council vote.

She wasn't really listening.

Nor did she care. The government never did anything for her anyway.

She was just getting ready to pour brown liquid into her cup when she heard a loud knock rattle the door.

BY T. STYLES

She wasn't accepting any tricks that day, so she was confused. Sighing deep, her fingers still wrapped around a freshly lit Newport she walked toward the sound and peered through the peephole. Next she grabbed the fully loaded .9mm at the door.

It was Giant.

Her heart dropped in irritation. His energy always meant trouble. She tucked the weapon in her stockings on the side of her hip, closed the robe and slowly she opened the door halfway, the chain still hooked.

"What you want?" She asked, squinting against the light behind him.

He licked his bottom lip, irritated already. "I just need to talk."

"About what?" She tapped ash off her cigarette. "You fired me remember? For getting too close to the girls," she laughed. "So what you want with me now?"

"It's about Lemon."

Angie rolled her eyes, then slammed the door. A second later, she unlatched the chain and opened it fully, stomping back to her spot on the couch like she regretted letting him in already. "Come on then."

He stepped inside. But he didn't sit. Just paced. "She been duckin' me," he said, tone already heated. "And I know you talk to her."

"I talk to a lotta people."

"I ain't talking about a lot of people, bitch," he said again, firmer. "I'm talking about her. Now tell me where she going next."

"What is your thing with her?" Angie narrowed her eyes. "I mean why you so obsessed with this girl?"

Giant dragged a hand down his face. "She owe me. Took off with my money. Broke agreements."

"Bullshit." Angie flicked her ashes with force. "You think I don't know what she brought in for you? I used to do your counts, remember? Lemon's debt been paid twice over."

Giant's jaw clenched, nostrils flaring. He said nothing.

Angie leaned forward, elbows to her knees, voice low and raspy. "But this ain't about money is it? Because we all know you got plenty."

He turned away, gaze darting over her dusty bookcase like it could explain what he couldn't say.

That's when Angie froze.

Her eyes glazed over, like something hit her spirit sideways.

She stood up and left the room without a word.

Giant frowned, confused.

Moments later she came back with a box...the kind folks used to keep old birthday cards and baby shoes inside. It was taped around the edges, stained with water damage. She sat back down and dropped it on the coffee table.

"Fuck is you doing?"

"You know, I ain't looked through this in years," she said as she peeled it open, pulled out a thick photo album with a wrinkled plastic cover. She flipped past old street shots, club nights, girls laughing on rooftops.

Then she paused. "Damn," she whispered.

She pulled out a photo, the edges curled and tacky with age. A younger Giant, maybe in his early 20s, smiling...not that hard, ego-wrapped smile he wore now, but a soft one. From back in the day when they were all friends. His arm was around a girl with gold skin and honey eyes, lips full and smiling, with a cascade of yellow-streaked hair that danced in the light.

Angie turned the photo toward him. "You remember her?"

Of course he remembered her. Thought about her more often than he wanted to admit. So he just stared for a while, almost as if he could go back to that time.

Angie nodded to herself. "I see it now. She looks like Lisa."

Giant's throat bobbed.

"She was the one. Your first. Showed you how to make money selling pussy...real money. But you ain't want it at first, did you?" Angie didn't wait for his answer. "You wanted love. Thought you found it in her. But she left with your best friend and broke your heart. And you never been the same. Been taking your pain out on women ever since."

"Be careful."

"You already killed Lisa...why you punishing Lemon too? And everyone she loves."

His fists clenched, but he didn't move. "You see Lemon or not, bitch. I don't need no — "

"I ain't saying you love her," Angie said, softer now. "But I get it. You think hurting Lemon gonna undo what happened with Lisa? It ain't."

He paced more.

"And Hazel? For goodness sake she's just a baby. And you damn sure not gonna get back what you lost by destroying them."

Giant stood quiet, jaw wired shut. Still looking at the photo in her hand she forgot she was holding. Taking a deep breath, he turned and snatched the door open. "Wash your pussy, whore. I smell it from over here."

CHAPTER THIRTY-SEVEN

Rain clung to me like oil.

Yeah, I was back at that man's house. So the fuck what! Talking to this woman was on my list of to do's.

Water soaked through my coat and clung to the curls at the nape of my neck. My boots made soft splashes in the mud lining the edge of the walkway, but I didn't care. I wasn't here to be polite or clean or cautious.

Not anymore.

The porch light was on, and I walked past the door I once entered to go to the front.

I was done pretending.

I climbed the steps, the wood slick beneath my feet, and paused at the door. Through the frame, I could hear soft jazz.

I knocked.

Firm.

Once.

Then twice.

It took a moment before I saw movement behind the frosted pane. Then the door creaked open, and there she was.

Her.

The woman I'd seen the last time I was here. The one with the trench coat and the effortless beauty. She looked exactly like she belonged there, framed by golden light and hardwood floors, like the house had been built around her.

She blinked at me, confused I guess.

That's nice for her because I wasn't confused. I was crystal.

"Can I help you?" She asked, voice calm, like she wasn't standing across from someone soaked to the bone and burning inside.

"Yeah," I said. "You can." I took a step closer. I wasn't going to waste time. "I've been living in your basement."

Her face didn't move at first. Just that same curious expression, like I was joking. "Excuse me?"

"Your eyes tell me you heard me the first time."

"I mean are you at the wrong address?" She crossed her arms, leaning against the frame. "Because what you saying not funny."

"You hear me laughing?"

She looked doubtful. So I gave her the details.

"The toilet in the basement…when you flush it, it runs for three minutes straight before it shuts up. There's a corner in the ceiling above the laundry unit covered in what looks like black mold. Everything else up there is clean though, bone white. So you should really get it fixed before you kill somebody."

Her face changed.

Subtle. But it changed.

Something in her eyes narrowed, sharp.

"You know what…I'm so sick of you whores pulling up like I don't know about y'all bitches. How else you think I got this place? From selling braids and pussy and I don't mean mine. Now get the fuck off my property before you really get your feelings hurt and your chest blowed out, Lemon."

Wow…she even knew my name.

When I looked down I saw a silver .45 clutched in her designer manicured hand.

With that, I got the fuck on.

CHAPTER THIRTY-EIGHT

After I parked, I saw her before she saw me.

Same spot. Same posture. Elbows on knees, phone in hand, hood up like armor. Every Sunday morning she would visit her father's grave at the cemetery.

I had a car.

But sometimes I took the bus with her too. Not because I had to...but she said it was the same bus her father always took to go to the store across from his current resting place. And so when I remembered I would go with her.

Today I had a different purpose.

She didn't look up until I was halfway to the curb. But when she saw me, she rolled her eyes so hard I thought they might get stuck.

"Fuck," she said. "What you want with me now?"

I didn't flinch. Just sat beside her on the same concrete step we used to wait on together. Instead of speaking right away, I let the silence settle. "I forgive you, Sheree."

She side-eyed me. "Forgive me for fucking what?"

"For putting your hands on me."

234

That made her laugh. A real, from-the-belly laugh that echoed down the empty street. "That's what you call an apology?" She said, wiping her eyes. "If so it needs work."

I smiled, just a little. "I'm serious. You shouldn't have put your hands on me, but I get it. You were worried. I was in too deep with Giant, and you saw it before I did. Because he did it to you. Although you should've kept it real with me about your history with him."

"Like that would have changed your mind."

"We'll never know."

Silence.

"I shouldn't have done it. But...you right. I was scared for you. Giant is insane."

I thought about him calling my mother and trying to set me up while at the motel. I even thought about his wife and her being in on selling girls and knew she breathed not one lie. "I'm done with him."

She raised an eyebrow. "Mm-hmm. You've said that before."

"This time is different." I looked straight ahead, eyes locked on nothing. "He crossed a line with Hazel."

"How many he got left to cross?"

"None."

There was something final in my voice, and I think she heard it too, because she didn't joke this time. Just nodded slow. "Yeah...aight."

The bus was still a distant hum. A long way off. We had time. "I got a plan, cuz."

She looked at me sideways. "A plan for what? Because unless it's about money I ain't in it."

"It's a plan to end this. Maybe even get a little paper too."

Her mouth curved, but not into a smile. "And let me guess. You need my help."

I nodded once. "I always need you."

She didn't say yes. She didn't say no.

"Don't you want your revenge on this nigga?"

She looked at me like she was weighing everything...past, present, and whatever came next.

The bus turned the corner down the block, headlights flickering in the gray light.

We stood.

And I was still waiting on an answer.

CHAPTER THIRTY-NINE

I sat at the table in the far corner of the diner, right under the flickering light that buzzed every few seconds like it had a nervous tick. My elbows rested on the torn tablecloth hands clasped, pretending I had patience.

Let's just say I didn't.

What I found crazy was this.

Nobody had come to take my order…not the bubbly blonde at the register, not the grumpy man pouring coffee. That was on purpose. I had been told the manager would help me personally.

And the manager? None other than my mother.

She finally walked out from the back, apron tight around her waist, expression stiff as cement. Her lips were set in that fake line she used to hide real feelings. "No roses this time huh?"

I smiled. "Sit," I said softly.

She didn't move. Her eyes darted to the other tables, calculating.

I leaned back in the booth, looked right at her and said loud enough for the next table to hear, "Does anybody wanna hear how my mother forced me to fuck her boyfriend since I was twelve years old?"

She sat.

Quickly.

The shame cracked through her face. Suddenly I wasn't a game anymore.

She adjusted her apron like that could fix anything. Her voice came out low and tight. "What you want with me? Because thanks to you, I won't be working here much longer when they arrest me."

"Well I didn't stab the nigga."

"You might as well. All I know is whatever you said to Marco made shit worse not better."

"What time you get off?"

"Ten tonight. Why?"

I exhaled, kept my voice even. "I want to tell you something. And I want you to listen. I don't even want you to respond. I don't want excuses either. All I want is for you to listen. Can you do that?"

She gave a short, hesitant nod.

I stared at her…this woman who gave me life but never love.

"For the longest time, I couldn't figure it out. How you could let him disappear from your room after sex, only to be gone…sometimes for hours. I would wonder

BY T. STYLES

if you knew a man was laying claim to your daughter like I was just...just some sick offering. A gift to prove your loyalty. I thought maybe you were broken too. Maybe you were as much a victim as I was. Or...maybe you didn't know."

My voice cracked, and I swallowed it down.

Later for the soft shit.

"I really believed that. Up until you changed the locks on me when I needed you most. When I was trying to save a little girl...who reminds me so much of me."

She shifted in the seat.

Uncomfortable.

Good.

"I really thought you were a victim. But I was wrong. You had a choice. You still do."

"And what choice is that?"

"Tell the people what he did to me. Take my side. Choose me." I looked into her eyes, hoping for redemption. Hoping for love.

"The only victim around here is me."

"I told you not to talk," I got a bit louder. "Unless you want me to tell this whole place the raunchy details of my childhood."

A couple of waitresses turned toward us. My mother raised a shaky hand, palm out, begging me with her eyes.

I lowered my voice again. "I'm done. I don't want you to call me. I don't want to hear from you. Ever. Again."

She opened her mouth anyway. "First of all, I didn't even—"

"Does anybody want to hear how horrible of a person my mother is?" I raised my voice, cutting her off again.

More heads turned. When I looked back I saw far too many people wiping the same counter, staring in our direction. They wanted all the tea, and I was about to serve it hot.

I leaned in just enough for her to feel the chill in my breath. "Next time you won't be able to stop the shit coming out my mouth."

Her face collapsed into panic, but I wasn't done.

"You'll finally get what you deserve. And I will too." I stood up.

"May I talk now?"

I nodded.

She looked up at me, tried one last jab. "And what do I deserve?"

240   BY T. STYLES

"You'll see."

"And what do you deserve?"

"Better. Because the only thing worse than living without a mother... is living with a mother like you."

Mariah opened the door with one hand still clutching the knob, the other resting on her hip.

Lemon was on the other side.

Standing beside Mariah was Walker...broad, quiet, and serious-faced, his frame nearly filling the doorway behind her. He didn't say anything, just nodded hello to her once.

Lemon remained outside for a moment before stepping in. Her breath hitched as she crossed the threshold. She didn't make eye contact...not yet anyway. Too much was on her mind. Her fingers were twitching at her sides, her jaw tight. The door clicked shut behind her as she leaned against the wall.

"You sure you want to do this?" Mariah asked. Her voice was low but firm, like she was bracing for the answer.

Lemon's eyes moved from Mariah to Walker. Her lips parted but she didn't speak right away, just nodded slowly...once, then twice.

"Yeah," she said, as she looked at Walker. "Just don't kill me."

My mother's house smelled like old cigarettes and that cheap pine cleaner she used to buy. I kept my shades on...the kind with mirrored lenses so he couldn't see my eyes.

The moment I knocked, Marco opened the door squinting, like he was trying to place me. His shirt was stained per usual with his greasy ass. "Jay?" His voice cracked. "That you?"

I stepped inside, letting my lemon-yellow hair catch the light. "Who else would it be?"

"Your mama know you here?"

"Does it matter? She never stopped you in the past. Why stop you now?

He grinned. "Christmas coming early huh?" He gripped his dick. "I always knew you would be back. Told you and everything."

He did.

And he was right.

I walked past him toward the hallway. His breathing changed behind me. The bedroom was exactly how I remembered...queen bed with ashy black flannel sheets to hide the stains and shame.

Still I sat on the edge, the springs whining under my weight. He stood in the doorway, blocking the light. "You ain't said why you came yet."

I reached back, unhooked my halter top. Let it slide down to my waist. The scars from last month's client were still raised.

Seeing what I came for, his Adam's apple bobbed. "Shit...it's like that?"

The shades stayed on. He didn't ask why.

When he reached for his belt, I thought about the straight razor in my back pocket. How easy it'd be to carve that fat neck while he panted over me. But I had a plan I intended on seeing through.

The details didn't need to be rehashed. I had been with this monster many times before. Let's just say we had sex. And for the first time it was consensual.

LEMON

Well…at least he thought.

When it was over, I went to the bathroom but this time, I didn't cry like I had in the past. I wiped everything but my pussy. When I was done I moved past the bedroom and his fat ass was out cold.

So I walked through the living room, out the door and down the hallway. Once in my car I made a call an hour later. The exact time was important.

The police showed up a little while after and I parked down the block just enough for him to see me. It took a minute but before long he was pulled out in cuffs. My body trembled so much in delight I'm mad I didn't film it for later. It's fine though, I would remember it all my life.

When he looked my way, I flashed the lights.

He glared.

Checkmate bitch!

With him in cuffs for rape, I went to the hospital. They gave me a kit and when I was asked to remove my shades I did. I sat patiently as they took photos of the bruises on my face.

You have to understand, I was all in on this plan. I even had Walker hit me several times, which he didn't want to do until Mariah, and I begged him to perfect the look.

244   **BY T. STYLES**

It was a different kind of pain. One that would come with sweet revenge.

The rest was makeup. And when they attempted to touch my eye in those areas, I would wince. Eventually they left it alone and just took the pictures. When they were done, I stared at the ceiling until I heard another knock.

Two officers walked in. One of them held a clipboard and the other looked at me like I was already broken.

"So," the first one said, stepping closer to my bedside, "we understand Marco Ramirez did this to you."

I nodded slowly.

"At what time?"

I remembered my mother got off at 10 o'clock. So I stuck to the time I told him earlier which was about 10:45. Even though it was at about 9:30. This was the reason I waited until an hour after I left.

He glanced at his partner, then back at me. "Was there...anyone else involved?"

I hesitated. The air in the room thickened, pressing against my chest.

"Yes," I said quietly.

"Who?" He asked.

I took a breath, deep and shaky. The words tasted like blood and betrayal. "My mother hit me too after she saw him raping me. She blamed me."

CHAPTER FORTY

I was sitting cross-legged on the bed, notes scattered all around me like little pieces of a puzzle. Names, times, dates.

Marco was in jail. So was my mother for "assaulting me". And because she had already stabbed him things weren't looking too good for old girl. I was checking to see if I felt a way after it all went down, but fortunately I do not.

My mother was a mess.

She been a mess.

And so she deserved to be right where she was.

The thing was, Giant was still free, and Hazel...Hazel was still out there somewhere.

There wasn't room to rest. So I strapped on my heels and threw on my jacket when my phone buzzed. A restricted number. I froze.

Jail?

I answered. "Yeah?"

There was a pause. Then her voice, softer than I expected. Where was the notification letting me know an inmate was trying to reach me?

"Where are you?" I asked, hoping my plan worked.

"You know where I am. Baby...I don't know why you did this, but please tell the truth."

I closed my eyes. "I don't know what you talking about."

"You told the people what Marco did to you...that I was involved and hit you. For apparent bruises on your face. That's a lie."

"But you *were* involved," I said quietly, my voice cold. "And everybody at your job heard me talk to you about the past. Don't you remember?"

She gasped...I heard it clearly. "So you planned this?"

"Mother, the real question is why *you* lying?"

"I'm not lying," she insisted.

"You were involved in this, and you were involved from the moment I was twelve years old.

"Jaystar, don't say all of that on the phone."

I smiled.

She thought she was going to trap me in a lie when I was about to give them everything. "When you...when you let him first sneak into my room after he got done with you, all the way up to now, bitch," My words came out like ice. "Now, what do you want me to do? You have to face justice, sweetheart."

"Jaystar, I'm begging you," she said, voice trembling, "please drop the charges."

"It's rape...its beyond me now."

"That's not true. You can tell them you lied. Because I...I finally realize what his actions did to you. I finally realize I should've stepped up more... I should've protected you. I'm sorry. I'm so sorry it took this to make me see. But we can get it right. I know we can."

For a second, I felt it. That small crack in my chest. That ache that only a daughter feels when she hears her mother cry. Luckily for me she kept talking.

"If you could drop the charges on both of us... him and me that would be—"

That's when I smiled. Not because it was funny. But because it was right on time.

"Remember when I said you would get what you deserve? When we were at your job."

Silence.

"This is what I meant."

I hung up the phone and walked out the door.

CHAPTER FORTY-ONE

The bar was dim, lit mostly by a strip of blue LEDs that rimmed the counter and made everything glow a little cold. I sat between Mariah and Sheree, our half-drunk cocktails lined up like little stained-glass windows. My face still hurt from the solid that Walker did for me, allowing me to give my mother and her nigga exactly what they deserved.

Mariah slid another drink closer. "You sure you don't want one more?"

I shook my head and pushed it back gently. "Not tonight."

She breathed deeper. "Okay…let's get to it. I don't think it's safe," Mariah said, stirring the ice in her glass. "What you doing can backfire. Fast."

Sheree exhaled hard. "Normally, I'd be on your side, Jay."

I frowned. "On my side since when?"

She laughed. "Seriously…this is too dangerous. And it's not just dangerous for you…it's dangerous for everybody involved."

"Do you want out?" I asked her and then looked at Mariah. "Do you?"

"You know I'm in this to the end," Mariah said. "For what he did to you."

I looked at my cousin.

"And I'm still trying to get back at him for shooting me. So I'm in too."

Mariah gasped, never hearing that tea before.

"Then it's settled," I said.

I glanced across the bar, my fingers tightening slightly around my glass. The bartender was watching me again. Same squinted look, same smug glare like he had a secret to tell and was waiting on the right moment.

Oh…I remembered him now.

He was a client.

One of the worst ones too…who didn't pay, just vanished after pretending he would go to his car to get the money.

"I don't have a choice," I finally said, turning back to my girls. "This is the only way I can get information about Hazel. And I'm sooo…sooo confident it will work."

They both looked at me like I'd already gone too far. Maybe I had.

Sheree leaned in closer. "What if it's too late? Like what if…what if she's gone?"

"I don't believe that."

LEMON

Mariah rubbed her temple like it was throbbing. "And what if Giant knows you're coming? And is waiting to set you up."

"He thinks I'm weak. He'll learn I'm not."

When the bartender came I requested the check. When it arrived I poured the one drink I didn't finish on the floor.

"Girl, what you doing?" Mariah asked looking at me and then the bartender.

"It's not an issue, the entire tab is on him," I said to him. "Ain't I right."

He swallowed and nodded slowly.

I felt both Mariah and Sheree stare at me like I was different. Maybe it was because I am.

I drove to my old block because today I was looking for someone else.

I circled the neighborhood like a memory on loop until I found what I was looking for, the narrow alleyway between two worn-down buildings that always smelled like piss. And there they were.

252   **BY T. STYLES**

Leslie, Shawny, and Keisha.

Her friends.

Keisha was snapping her fingers in rhythm to whatever was blasting from the small speaker clipped to her waistband, laughing loud and open-mouthed. Shawny stood with one foot kicked up behind her like she posed for trouble. While Leslie leaned against the brick wall, arms folded, eyes darting all over me.

But something was different.

Their hair was freshly laid, nails done to perfection, and their outfits…tight, expensive, screaming cash. Real cash. Not the kind you save up babysitting or bagging groceries. And not from working overnight shifts at no store either. Besides, they were all babies.

Nah, they had the kind of look that only came from one place. They were being compromised.

Did Giant grab them too?

I parked and got out, slamming my car door with more force than necessary.

Leslie and Keisha flinched.

I can tell they were about to run because I saw it in the way their bodies tensed but I raised my voice before they could bolt. "Don't do it!"

They froze.

"I mean it," I continued, walking toward them.

LEMON

All three turned to face me.

Shawny cocked her head like she was unimpressed, Keisha folded her arms and Leslie looked everywhere but at me.

"You know," I said, eyes bouncing between them, "when I first came around asking about Hazel, I didn't see what was right in front of me."

Shawny raised an eyebrow. "And what's that supposed to mean?"

I gave her a small, joyless smile. "Where y'all getting money?"

That got them.

Shawny glanced at Leslie and then narrowed her eyes at me. Always the mouthpiece, she spoke first. "Why you worried? It ain't none of your business."

Leslie looked down, lips tight, guilt blooming like a bruise across her face.

I took another step forward. "Look, I'm not playing games with 'nair one of y'all. Whatever y'all got going on, that's on you. I ain't your mama." I paused. Let the weight of my words hit the air. "But you gonna give me the information I want or I'm blowing shit up. I hope by now y'all know I'm serious."

BY T. STYLES

A meeting was in session.

Lemon stood in the center of Mariah's living room, facing the group seated on the couch. The weight of the moment hung heavy in the air.

Mariah leaned against the wall near the kitchen, arms crossed tightly over her breasts. While Sheree sat at the edge of a cushioned chair, tapping her foot.

Leslie, Shawny, and Keisha were spread across the sofa, their postures ranging from annoyed to scared.

"Are y'all ready?" Lemon asked the girls, her voice steady, but her nerves evident in the way her fingers curled into her palms.

Shawny gave a half nod. "We gonna do it but I'm not feeling it," she said with an attitude.

"What you mad for?" Mariah cut in, her eyebrow raised. "Ain't like y'all not still getting paid."

Shawny rolled her eyes hard, the lip gloss on her mouth catching the light. "Because we don't want our bag messed with after this over."

"I'm sorry if I'm not clear, if your money tied to Giant, it's over now," Lemon said seriously. "What I'm giving you is paper I been saving for another reason. And we wouldn't even be talking to y'all about this if you weren't already mixed in. Now if you're scared let me know."

Shawny leaned forward. "Y'all just think we some young, dumb girls. But we know what we doing when we be out in the streets."

"Do you though?" Lemon said sharply, stepping forward. Her voice wasn't loud, but it was serious. "Because even if it's not Giant, unless y'all figure out that this ain't the way…he won't be the last man who takes advantage."

Keisha's face twisted. "What happened to you ain't got nothin' to do with us, Jay."

Sheree's voice sharpened. "Meaning?"

Shawny shrugged, arms folded. "You know what she mean. We heard about the kind of relationship you had. You and your mama…with her boyfriend."

"Fuck is you talking about?" Lemon continued.

"Wasn't y'all in a threesome type of situation?"

The room went dead quiet.

Lemon didn't flinch, but the words hit her like thrown rocks.

Before she could respond, Mariah spoke up, firm and controlled. "If you knew so much, then you'd know that when

256

you young, you not able to consent. That's how Jay started out. Just like none of y'all can consent when Giant be trying to get y'all to do whatever the fuck he got going on, young ass hoes."

"Exactly, so all this judgmental shit need to stop," Sheree added. "Six months back I found a young girl like you cut in half. Separated by the stomach. Guts hanging out for her mother to identify later. So you may wanna be a bit more humble."

Keisha looked down. Leslie's jaw tightened and Shawny stayed defiant, but the bite in her voice dimmed.

"At the end of the day," Mariah added, "he's going down. You can either go down with him, which I know y'all ain't ready for, or you can help us."

Lemon took a breath. "I know y'all not feelin' me right now. I get it. But one day, you'll be glad I stepped in. Because I wish someone would've stepped in for me."

Another breath.

"Now, do y'all remember your lines or what?" Sheree said, sick of all of their young asses.

I walked into the police station, the chill of the air conditioning biting through my thin jacket. It wasn't my first time here, but this time felt different. This time, I wasn't here to beg...I was here to make something move.

Confident about my pending plan I stepped up to the front desk. The officer behind the glass didn't even look up at first. "Can I speak to a detective?"

His eyes moved toward mine...skeptical like. Especially after observing my bruised face. "What's this about?"

"Missing girls."

He frowned. Deep lines settled across his forehead as he looked me up and down, like I might be wasting his time. Then he rose and walked away without another word.

Fifteen minutes passed.

I sat in one of those plastic waiting chairs, the kind that scrape the back of your legs if you shift wrong. My knee bounced with impatience until I heard footsteps.

Two officers appeared...a Black woman, older, maybe late forties, with stern eyes and a badge that sat like a burden on her chest. The other, a white man in his

BY T. STYLES

thirties, tall and tired looking, like he'd been through too many bad nights and not enough justice.

"What's going on?" The woman asked me.

I stood up, wiping my palms down the sides of my jeans. "I called you guys before...about Nathaniel 'Giant' Lee."

The woman's jaw twitched. "We know who Giant is."

"Well, he's taking three girls to a fight party. Tonight."

The man raised a brow, his arms crossing casually. "And?"

"They're young. Under thirteen even. And I'm afraid that what he has planned will do more harm than good."

The woman narrowed her eyes at me. "You came here before, didn't you?"

"Yes," I said slowly. "But...I didn't meet with you."

"That don't mean we don't know you."

Silence.

"They said you were adamant then," she said, "about having information on him in the past. But that you couldn't follow through."

The man leaned in and looked deeper at me. "Are you sure you can follow through now?"

I didn't blink. Didn't flinch. "I promise you will get what you want tonight. Now are y'all gonna help me? Or are y'all on this nigga's payroll?"

BY T. STYLES

CHAPTER FORTY-TWO

The night sky meant the young women no good.

Shawny, Leslie, and Keisha stood in a crooked huddle on the block outside of their apartment complex. The streetlight flickered above them, shining a glow over cracked sidewalks and the graffiti-tagged mailbox.

The night air bit through their thin jackets, but they didn't seem to mind. Each of them wore tights, short skirts, or fitted jeans, clothes more suited for a club than a cold Baltimore evening. From a distance, they might've looked like young women trying too hard to be grown. But up close, it was impossible to ignore that they were just little girls playing dress up.

A black Mercedes Sprinter pulled up with quiet menace, when they peered inside they saw Giant in the back, his eyes hidden behind tinted windows. The passenger door cracked open, and a man in all black stepped out and wordlessly opened the sliding door for the girls.

Shawny was the first to hop inside, already gushing like she was losing the plot. This wasn't about fun.

This was about having a mission.

"Damn, this car nice." Her voice was bold, loud and annoying as fuck.

Leslie, quieter by nature and clutching her phone tightly, followed. Once inside, she sat in the corner and subtly hit the record button, her thumb trembling slightly. She was the one friend that understood how important this was.

She knew this whole setup wasn't about partying...it was about catching Giant trying to traffic them. And maybe even save Hazel, her friend. She was also trying to hit the button on the phone to share locations with Lemon and Sheree, but it wasn't working. The weight of it pressed down on her chest.

If Lemon didn't know where they were, what was to stop them from showing up missing?

While Leslie continued to try to work, Keisha slid in last, her eyes scanning the Sprinter's sleek interior while she fiddled with her jacket zipper. With the three girls trapped, the doors slid shut, and the Sprinter began to glide away from the curb.

No one said anything for a while...not Giant, not the passenger, not the driver. The silence stretched long and tight.

Until the great lip flapper got to talking.

"Y'all really takin' us to a fight party?" Shawny said, trying to fill the space. "And lettin' us work? Like, for real?"

"Why else would you be here?"

She was so goofy acting that Leslie was almost confused. Did she remember what they were supposed to be doing?

Shawny turned to her friends, all smiles. "Y'all ready?"

BY T. STYLES

Leslie swallowed hard. Keisha didn't answer.

Then Giant spoke, his voice low but sharp. "You talk too much. So sit back and shut the fuck up before I let you see something."

Shawny blinked. "What you just say?"

"You too grown for your own good," he snapped.

Shawny glared. "Too grown! But ain't that the fucking point?" She mumbled. "Because you — "

"I said, shut up, young bitch. Before I make you bleed."

Now she knew he was serious.

Deathly serious.

A few moments later, they pulled into a parking lot behind a brick apartment building with many wood covered windows. Giant was waiting to pick up another girl, and so the plan was for them all to walk into his friend Larron's house.

But the girls were confused. They thought they were all going to the party now.

Shit was already going off plan.

For some reason, Leslie still couldn't activate the location's button for Lemon. And there was no time to do anything because when the driver stepped out and opened their door, it was clear it was time to move.

"Come on, girl," the driver said.

Leslie hesitated, then followed, her phone still clutched in her palm. The driver trailed behind her.

Still inside the Sprinter, Giant stepped out and bent down to help Shawny and Keisha gather the lip glosses, combs, and compact mirrors they had scattered everywhere while doing makeup during the ride.

That's when the blue and white police cruiser pulled up.

It rolled in slow, headlights off until it got close.

How did they know where Giant would be?

The same female officer who hadn't taken Lemon seriously at the precinct climbed out of the driver's side. Her eyes swept over the scene...Giant, the van, the girls.

She stepped up to them, hand near her belt. "Evening. Mind telling me how you know these girls?"

Giant rose his chin. "Is there a problem?"

"Yes, I'm still waiting on my answer."

He shifted a little and suddenly didn't seem so brave. "They asked for a ride," he said smoothly, too smoothly. "Said they liked the van. So I gave them one."

The officer's eyes didn't budge. "That so?"

Shawny, catching the tension and sensing what was coming, piped up quickly. "Yeah, we did. We just wanted to ride in it seeing as though it's a Mercedes." She looked back at it and then at them. "I mean, it's nice, right?"

BY T. STYLES

Keisha nodded beside her, though her arms were wrapped tight across her chest now.

The officer looked at them carefully. "You girls know someone named Hazel?"

The air got thick. Especially thick when Shawny and Keisha looked to find Leslie and noticed she was already gone.

Shawny was the one to speak again. "Hazel? Nah, we don't know no Hazel."

The officer paused, then exhaled. "Alright. Y'all need to come with me then. I'll give you a ride back home."

Shawny looked like she wanted to say more, but Keisha had already started walking toward the cop car. But what about Leslie?

"Are you waiting for anything?" The officer asked her.

She was about to tell them about her friend, but when she glanced at Giant she knew if she did, she would die. So along with Keisha she climbed into the back of the police cruiser, doors clicking shut behind them.

As they drove off, Giant stood in place, jaw clenched so tight it looked like he might break a tooth. He had already received money for them...all three really. And now he would have to pay it back. The red and blue lights flashed once before fading out as the cruiser drove away.

Giant was livid.

CHAPTER FORTY-THREE

My phone rang so loud, I almost dropped it into my lap as I handled the steering wheel. I was already driving too fast, windows cracked, and my dreads shaken dizzy. My nerves were shot, and I hadn't eaten anything but a granola bar since morning.

Then the name flashed across the screen: **Shawny**.

My stomach turned.

I answered on the second ring.

"Shawny, is everything okay?"

Her voice came through like thunder. Panicked. Breathless. "Jay! Jay, it didn't work out. Something is wrong!"

My foot jerked as I slammed the brake, swerved too hard.

A car honked so loud behind me I thought it was gonna run straight through my windshield. So I pulled over crooked on the shoulder, heart pounding so fast I could hear it in my ears.

"What you mean something went wrong?" I snapped. "What the hell you talking about?"

"He has her," Shawny cried. "Giant...he has Leslie. I don't know where, I don't know why, but he has her."

266

For a second, the world stopped.

Everything. The cars. The air. My breath.

It felt like my whole chest collapsed on itself.

Not Leslie. Not her.

I had set the plan. I had pulled the strings. This was supposed to expose him, not... whatever the hell this was.

"Where did you last see her?" I asked, trying to keep my voice from cracking.

"At an apartment building!" Shawny said, sobbing harder. "But...but I heard him talking about going to a big house. That they had to pick up some other girls first. I think that's why we were there!"

"What is he up to?" I said to myself.

"We got separated, and next thing I knew...the cops...the car...I mean..."

My hand trembled as I held the phone to my ear. She was still talking but I couldn't hear her anymore. All this was my fault. I should've never involved them. They were just kids playing in a grown man's game.

A game I'd barely survived myself.

I pressed the heel of my hand to my forehead, trying to stop the room from spinning even though I wasn't in a room at all.

"Okay," I said finally. She was still crying. "Okay…okay…are you home?"

"Yes."

"Good…I need you to stay there. Where is Keisha?"

"She's at home too." She cried a bit louder. "Jay, I'm…I'm scared. I think he knows we were trying to set him up. What if he comes for me too?"

"I won't let that happen," I promised, even though I didn't know how the hell I'd keep it. "Just hang tight. I'm going to find her."

She sniffled. "What if you can't?"

I didn't answer.

Because I didn't know.

And because even thinking about that possibility was enough to crush the last strong part of me left.

When the call ended, I sat there. Car idling. Guilt sitting heavy in my lap. The streetlights blinked against the windshield, and all I could think was that I had traded her safety for a plan.

And then there was the police. How did they know where Giant would be? I couldn't get the tab on Leslie's locations like planned. So how did they know?

Then it dawned on me, they probably in on it too.

And now two of my girls are missing.

Giant's house party was underway but not everyone got a formal invite.

Mariah and Sheree stepped out of the Uber and onto the freshly paved driveway like they belonged there.

It was the kind of house people pretended not to envy...big and modern. Since the noise was at a minimum, it made them wonder how much money was spent to keep sound inside. The sprawling Baltimore County mansion had a long wraparound porch, wide glowing windows, and enough cars parked up and down the street to suggest something major was happening.

And it was.

Outside, the crowd spilled across the lawn like beer foam...mostly men, loud and wild, flashing smiles and jewels most couldn't afford. Music pulsed from inside, deep and bassy, swallowing half the conversations around it. A few women posed on the front steps for pictures. Others smoked in small, glammed-up circles, their dresses loud, their lashes louder, their bodies banging.

Mariah adjusted the hood of her camel coat. Beneath it she looked the part, and her makeup was flawless, hair laid like silk. Sheree had on a black leather mini dress and an attitude sharp enough to slice glass. They looked good, expensive.

Still, they didn't come to be seen.

They came to see.

They eased into the sea of bodies, brushing past men who threw out their best lines. Some drunk, some charming, all of them ignored as they moved on the way to the door.

They weren't rude, just on a mission.

When they made it close to the front door, Sheree gripped Mariah's wrist, to stop her from going into his eyeline.

There he was…Giant.

Just inside so they had to duck out the way so they wouldn't be spotted.

He was leaning against the side of the house, flashing that easy smile at one of the men, while collecting a wad of folded bills like it was nothing. The moment hung like a too-tight shoe but before he could spot them because there was nowhere else to hide, someone called his name from the back. He disappeared inside and up the staircase without looking their way.

Perfect timing.

They slipped inside.

The house was even louder than the outside, crowded with shoulder-brushing guests and a haze of smoke so thick it

BY T. STYLES

burned the eyes. Big screens lined the walls, each playing undercard bouts.

It was a mess.

A girl in a red dress was passed out on the leather couch, surrounded by empty cups and greedy stares. Nobody helped her opting to watch instead.

Unfortunately she wasn't their problem. Instead, Mariah and Sheree moved carefully, sticking close to the walls while staying in character.

Every now and again they'd whisper to each other when they could, noting what they saw...too many locked doors, too many men looking for girls too young to be there, too many signs that Lemon might've been right.

"What if Hazel's really here?" Sheree asked quietly.

They split briefly, their phones stayed in hand, ready to record or call, whichever had to happen first. It was an hour of weaving through music, sweat, perfume, and paranoia.

And then Walker walked inside.

Six foot two, built like a linebacker, dark skinned with a hoodie pulled over his head and heat in his walk. He didn't say a word.

But Mariah knew her man anywhere.

When he spotted her she nodded.

And Walker nodded back.

For now they had to keep their distance as it was obvious that something was about to go down.

Walker slipped into the party like he belonged there.

He had been watching for a while...long enough to see how things worked. How one man whispered something to Giant by the staircase, and a moment later, received a small paper ticket and a nod toward the roped-off stairs where another man let him inside.

That's where the real party was.

So Walker approached with a calm confidence, hands loose at his sides. "I'm looking for something special," he said.

Giant didn't flinch. Just stared at him. Assessing. "Special's reserved."

"I know what it is, nigga," Walker continued, unfazed. "You got something for me or not?"

Giant's eyes narrowed and Walker said nothing. Instead, he reached into the inside of his jacket and pulled out a fat roll of cash, held tight with a worn tan rubber band. He didn't wave it around. He didn't offer it yet. Just showed it.

That got a reaction.

272

Giant's stance shifted, barely...but it was enough. *"Now what you looking for again?"*

"Your best. Young."

For a moment, neither moved. Then Giant leaned forward, eyes gleaming with something between respect and suspicion. *"You police?"*

Walker glared and the look made Giant know he hated the cops as much as himself. *"If you playing games, I will kill you."*

"Same here."

With an understanding, they disappeared upstairs.

Mariah and Sheree stood near the mirrored wall, their drinks untouched, eyes trailing Walker as he disappeared up the staircase behind Giant. The moment he vanished from view; Sheree's phone buzzed with a message from Lemon.

A single word: **Here**.

They moved quickly, quietly, slipping past the velvet curtain and heading toward the service hallway. When they cracked open the back door, a gust of cool air rushed in, and Lemon stepped through.

She looked sharp, determined. Her eyes darted over their shoulders toward the noise inside.

"You were right," Mariah said, her voice low.

Sheree nodded, glancing down. "About all of it."

Lemon didn't slow her stride. "Let's not get too excited just yet," she whispered.

Mariah and Sheree shared a look, then pointed up.

Lemon's eyes followed the gesture to the top of the stairs, where shadows pooled and the real party...whatever it was...was underway. "I'm going up there."

Sheree grabbed her cousin's arm. Her voice cracked. "Let's call the police before — ."

"I'm sick of calling them niggas and not getting help. I'ma wait until it's the right time."

"And what time is that?"

"Maybe it's when I have his blood on my hands."

Sheree took a deep breath. "Just...be safe, okay?"

Lemon's face softened, just for a moment. Then she pulled Sheree into a hug and whispered, "Unfortunately, that's the last thing on my mind." Without another word, she turned and disappeared into the crowd, moving like someone with nothing left to lose.

BY T. STYLES

Walker followed Giant down a narrow hallway soaked in shadow. Carpet muffled their footsteps, but not the sounds. Behind closed doors, there were soft noises…whispers, laughter, moans. The thump of the bass from downstairs still bled through the ceiling above them.

Walker kept his expression neutral, eyes scanning the doors they passed. Each was numbered with yellow post its.

Giant stopped in front of one near the end of the hall, number 18, and opened it without a word. Inside, the lighting was low and warm, and a young black woman sat perched on the edge of a velvet loveseat, legs crossed, hands resting neatly on her lap.

She was smiling, ready to serve.

Her features were soft, her eyes curious.

She was an adult but still gave off that too-young impression…too eager, too rehearsed.

Walker stepped in slowly, scanning the room like he was checking for cameras. He gave her a polite nod, the kind that says "I see you" without commitment.

Then he turned to Giant. "She's not who I'm looking for."

Giant's head tilted slightly. Not confusion…just a rising alertness. "You looking for someone in particular? Because you didn't say that shit."

"Not specific…I meant young."

Giant growled. "This is young."

"I need something else," Walker said calmly, firmly. "Someone younger."

A beat passed. Then two.

Giant's eyes narrowed. "Take it or leave it, nigga. 'Cause either way you not getting your money back."

Before Walker could respond, the door slammed shut behind him. And the woman rose watching him carefully. Her smile had faded, replaced by something more uncertain.

"I'm not good enough?"

"Shawty, it's not even about that shit."

Lemon moved fast but quiet.

With Giant nowhere in sight…distracted somewhere deeper in the house…she took her chance. The hallway upstairs was longer than she expected, with branches that twisted into dim corridors and closed doors.

BY T. STYLES

She pushed through them one by one.

Some were empty. Some weren't. Some doors creaked open to confused faces, flushed skin, too much perfume and not enough consent. More than once, voices barked at her... "What the hell?" or "Get the fuck out!" ...but Lemon didn't stop. She didn't even flinch.

She was looking for Hazel.

She was looking for Leslie.

The hallway at the back was darker, quieter. Could they be there? Lemon paused at the last door, heart racing, and turned the knob. Inside, the light was dim, but not dark enough to hide the damage.

Her heart dropped.

Leslie was there...crumpled on the floor beside a chaise, her makeup smeared, her dress torn at the strap. Her arms were wrapped around herself like she was trying to hold something in or keep herself together.

She had been given a substance that much Lemon was certain.

Devastated, Lemon dropped to her knees.

"Leslie," she whispered, wrapping her arms around her while examining her body too. "I'm sorry. God, I'm so sorry. I should've never let you out of my sight."

Leslie shook in her arms but didn't speak. Her silence was louder than anything. She was possibly drugged because something was wrong. Thinking on her feet, despite not finding Hazel, Lemon pulled out her phone with a shaking hand and dialed 911.

When the operator answered, she gave the address, her name, and said the words clearly: "There's a man who's been trafficking women. Young girls. I have one with me and she's unconscious. You need to come now and don't fuck up this time! I'm sick of y'alls asses!"

Then she tucked the phone away and brushed hair from Leslie's face. "I'm coming back. Just stay here."

Leslie shook her head faintly, eyes barely open. "Don't...don't leave me."

"I gotta find Hazel. But I'll be back for you." Needing that to be an understanding, Lemon ran out the door.

She had to move quickly before Giant found out or the police arrived. So she checked the other rooms again, tearing through them faster now. She didn't care if people screamed or swore as she violated their privacy.

She was on her last door when she spotted something she had seen before. Hanging on a chair in one of the empty rooms was a dress.

Pink. Short.

It was Hazel's. The one she found in the closet during one of the last times she'd seen her. Proof she was there, Lemon reached out and touched it. The fabric was slightly damp.

278   **BY T. STYLES**

She closed her eyes for a breath. Hazel had been here. Recently.

But where was she now?

Was she gone? Taken? Hiding?

She didn't know. But she knew one thing, she couldn't leave Leslie behind. So she sprinted back down the hall toward the room and luckily Leslie was still there, trying to sit up, shaky but awake.

And that's when the doorway darkened.

Giant stood there.

His jaw was clenched, shoulders wide enough to block the hall behind him. His eyes burned into Lemon like he'd known it was her all along.

"Fuck is you doing in my house, bitch?"

But then something shifted. Distantly, like a ripple through the walls, came the wail of sirens. She could tell Giant heard it too be 'cause his head turned toward the sound.

He bolted out the door.

The hospital lights were too bright. Too clean. Too still.

Lemon sat between Sheree and Mariah in the waiting room, her shoulders stiff, her hands clenched in her lap. Around them, the white noise of grief...muffled voices, rustling clothing and the occasional sound of someone crying behind a tissue.

While they were waiting to see if Leslie would be okay, the police were working Giant's secret house.

Everyone, the women too, and even the men who used Giant's services had given their statements to the police hours ago. To save themselves they told it all, child. Every detail. Every face. Every name. In the end a warrant had been issued for Giant's arrest.

And in a twist none of them had seen coming, his wife...who'd been laughing and sipping champagne at the fight party, had also been arrested on-site. She was complicit. Embedded. Part of the whole machine.

But Giant was still out there so if they didn't have him, it wasn't good enough for Lemon.

With multiple I told y'all bitches so, the cops admitted that they were close to finding him. She didn't believe not a one.

Right now Lemon, Sheree and Mariah were waiting. Not just for justice. But for a good status on Leslie.

Leslie's family had arrived in waves. Aunts, cousins, an older brother who hadn't let go of the rosary in his hands since

280   **BY T. STYLES**

he walked through the doors. They filled the chairs and lined the walls with a silence that felt ready to explode.

A few of them gave Lemon the evil eye but Mariah and Sheree sat fearlessly protective, letting them know it was she who found her in the first place, while leaving out the part that she would never have been there if she didn't suggest or needed to find Hazel.

Then the doctor stepped into the waiting room, face drawn tight.

Lemon knew before he spoke.

"I'm sorry," he said, voice low and clear. "We did everything we could. But Leslie didn't make it."

The words hung in the air like ash.

Someone screamed. Someone fell. Lemon didn't know if it was Mariah, Sheree or one of Leslie's cousins. She couldn't hear anymore. Everything around her dropped into silence. Even her own heartbeat felt distant.

In a daze of rage, she stood up and walked away, down the corridor...and then out the door.

No one stopped her. She didn't explain. Didn't look back either.

The hospital doors opened, spilling her into the cold, gray light of early morning. Lemon didn't care. She was going to find him and take his fucking life.

CHAPTER FORTY-FOUR

S he beat the rain but it didn't matter.

Because Lemon knew something was off before she even reached the front door. It wasn't the silence. The old brickhouse where she rented a room was usually quiet. It was a solid build that meant whatever you wanted to do behind one of its six-bedroom doors would remain a secret.

This was different.

Nah, as her long cream-colored legs moved toward the building, a sense of dread took over her soul. It worsened when she opened the door and was unpleasantly surprised.

It was the smell.

Warm, metallic, like burnt plastic and something sweet gone bad. A thick scent that stuck to the back of her throat forcing her to relive the odor every time she swallowed.

Her door, the one upstairs, toward the side hallway where her neighbor Victor loved to sneak women in while cheating on his wife, was cracked open. When she looked down, she saw a patch of red hair caught in the latch.

"What...what is this?" She frowned.

Her mind went on a tour as she looked at the strands trying to determine the owner. She didn't know anyone with red hair. And when she pushed the door wider, more hair fell onto her damp doorway. Picking it up, she noticed it was clumped up.

Was it burned?

She was now sure the hair was synthetic which would account for the odor.

The next thing she felt was water sloshing at the heels of her shoes, seeping on the soles of her feet. Her cheap rug was dark and heavy with liquid, curling at the edges like it wanted to escape.

"Fuck is this?" After some research and a headache that would not let her go, she noticed the sink was on in her bedroom. Not just running...pouring. "Who...been in here?"

Wanting to understand while also being afraid, she stepped deeper inside, slow and careful.

The water had overflowed onto the counter. Her combs, the cheap bottle of edge control, the shea butter she rationed, and her makeup was all swimming in liquid.

But nothing was taken.

Just water pouring over everything she cherished plus the red clumpy hair.

And then she turned toward the bed.

And froze.

There, on the pillow, was more hair. Picking it up, she felt as if the floor had dropped from up under her.

Because she knew exactly what it meant now.

LEMON   283

Lemon hadn't been inside her old apartment building in a while, but it still carried the kind of scent memory could never erase…dust, old fried food, and betrayal baked into the walls.

When she saw the red hair in the doorframe of her room that was all she needed. Instantly she recalled the story Hazel told her about the costume her mother gave her, and how it was the only thing special she had ever given her.

So when she went to her room, the hair being left didn't feel like a warning. It felt like a message.

And Lemon was done ignoring signs.

Once at the building, her feet moved fast up the steps, past the old door to the left that once held memories of her mother and Marco. But this time she didn't pause.

She turned right.

To Hazel's old apartment.

With her hand on the knob, the door creaked open, because once again it was not locked. The hallway inside was dim, but what she saw froze her breath.

There she was…Hazel.

284 **BY T. STYLES**

The person she was ready to risk it all for. Looking at how small she appeared, she finally understood why Mariah said she was really attempting to save herself. The younger version of herself who needed help, and no one came.

Except, she knew that the outcome would be different.

Sitting in the corner on the floor, knees pulled to her chest, face stained with tears. Her hair now a jagged, red weave install that was uneven and looked like it had been thrown together in a rush. She didn't look thirteen. She looked used.

And then there was Giant...he was legit surprised to see her.

"So that bitch did tell you we would be here?" He looked at her and back at Lemon. "How when I took your phone?"

"What are you even doing here?" Lemon asked as her eyes remained on Hazel, as she desperately tried to think of a way to get her out.

"He was hiding from police," Hazel said softly. "So I told him we could hide out in your room. I snuck us in through the secret entrance in the back. Said I had to use the bathroom and that's when I burned my hair. But somebody saw him and said the city was looking for him. So I — ."

"Told him about your empty apartment."

Hazel nodded. "A place I used to come back to, hoping you would find me. But you never did."

Lemon broke inside. "I'm here now."

Although trembling, Hazel smiled.

"Shut the fuck up," he warned Hazel. "I should've never trusted your funky ass."

He was the same man he always was…grimy and filled with arrogance. But tonight, Lemon didn't flinch. She didn't cry. And she didn't run.

"I was right," Lemon said, her voice steady, each word striking like steel. "You just like every other man I've ever known. You take what you want and don't give a fuck about what's left."

Giant pushed himself off the wall, his movement lazy, taunting.

"But I'm not afraid of you anymore," Lemon continued, stepping closer to him.

Hazel's sobs thickened behind her.

"I stood up to Marco. I stood up to my own mother. And now I'm standing up to you."

He lunged toward her. Threat looming but Lemon didn't budge. Even as he came toe-to-toe with her, she leaned in. "You don't scare me, nigga. And I'm leaving here with Hazel."

Suddenly, the flash of metal in her hand.

The crack of impact pressing into flesh. She stabbed him in the gut. He didn't even realize what happened until his knees gave out and the room spun. In pain and confused, he stumbled backward and hit the ground hard. His fingers peddled his own blood. When he was down she stabbed him again, once, twice and again for good measure.

Hazel screamed at the horror.

But Lemon just stood still, breathing heavy, holding the handle tight. Giant groaned...his breath ragged. Then suddenly he stopped moving. Before long Hazel rushed to her side, trembling but for the first time feeling safe.

She had warned him that she would ruin his life if he hadn't handed over Hazel.

Now she made good on her threat.

Together, they stood over him. One broken. One bruised. Both reclaiming the strength stolen from them. Sirens howled in the distance, growing louder, splitting the quiet open like cake.

Covered in blood and wanting to make sure he was dead, Lemon kept her gaze on him. And when she saw his lids slack and unmoving, she whispered:

"You won't hurt her. Or anyone else. Ever again," Lemon said before reaching for Hazel's hand.

"I'm so sorry, Hazel. This was not the way. I should have never got in this lifestyle and put you in it. I was just – ."

"You didn't give up on me!" She said before gripping her around her waist. "And you remembered the story I told you

*about my mama. And the red hair. I knew you would," she
cried harder. "I knew you would."*

BY T. STYLES

EPILOGUE

*T*he television screen flickered softly in the background, placing a faint bluish glow over the living room. Lemon and Hazel were curled up on opposite ends of a cozy gray sectional, legs stretched out beneath a shared throw blanket. Both of them were on their phones, aimlessly scrolling...Hazel giggling at something on TikTok, Lemon clearing out messages she no longer felt obligated to return.

The scent of warm cinnamon and popcorn filled the air. A movie waited patiently on pause.

After doing her click business, Hazel sat her phone on the armrest. "You ready?"

Lemon smiled, placing her own phone face down on the coffee table too. She had enrolled back in college and was letting her new boss know at the cell phone company that she would need Thursdays off. He was able to oblige.

"Yep, let's do it."

The townhouse fell through due to the money she spent trying to find Hazel. Along with the money she gave in Leslie's honor. So an apartment would have to do. No worries though because their place was small, but it was theirs. It was clean, quiet, and safe and they could sleep at night.

The walls wore soft art prints and dollar store affirmations framed like gold. A sunbeam quilt Hazel had helped sew was slung over the back of the couch, and the fridge hummed in the kitchen...a subtle reminder of normalcy.

They had made it, even though Hazel never gave Lemon the details about her time with Giant, she made sure she attended counseling, something Hazel argued about at first.

Lemon had fought hard through courtrooms, trauma, and doubt...but in the end, she got custody of Hazel. And she intended to never let her down again.

The world kept moving and so had justice.

Giant may have been dead, but his wife received five after young girls testified against her...it was a lesser sentence, but enough to change her life and lessen that ego.

Marco, whose crimes extended beyond what Lemon ever imagined, had been handed fifteen years after other young women came forward with their stories.

Even her mother had faced time, three years for stabbing Marco and five years for luring girls to him whenever he wanted something younger. Her mother's assault charges from Lemon were dropped but Lemon didn't feel after the new charges that much more needed to be done.

The truth finally rose like cream to the top.

BY T. STYLES

Lemon didn't keep in touch with her mother. Hazel didn't keep in touch with hers either. And for once, neither of them felt guilty about it.

Just as the movie's opening scene began to roll, she heard a knock.

When Lemon stood up with a grin she was excited when she opened the door and saw the familiar faces of her best friend and her cousin. Both carried snacks...Mariah with two bottles of wine and Sheree with a bag full of corner store candy.

"Where's Walker?" Lemon asked.

Mariah rolled her eyes with a smirk. "We broke up. Again."

Lemon chuckled and held the door wider. "Good. I needed a girls' night anyway."

After the hugs they all settled in, laughter spilling over the sounds of the movie like background music. Pillows were thrown, candy passed around, and stories shared.

No judgment.

Just joy.

It wasn't perfect.

But it was freedom.

Women, finally standing up for one another.

Finally...enjoying the peace they made for themselves.

And the love they had for each other, as fragrant as a bag of lemons.

FROM

MEN

TO

MONSTERS

DIG YOUR OWN GRAVE

T. STYLES

CARTEL PUBLICATIONS

PRESENTS

The Cartel Publications Order Form

www.thecartelpublications.com

Inmates **ONLY** receive novels for $14.00 per book **PLUS**
shipping fee **PER BOOK.**
(Mail Order **MUST** come from inmate directly to receive
discount)

Shyt List 1	_____	$15.00
Shyt List 2	_____	$15.00
Shyt List 3	_____	$15.00
Shyt List 4	_____	$15.00
Shyt List 5	_____	$15.00
Shyt List 6	_____	$15.00
Pitbulls In A Skirt	_____	$15.00
Pitbulls In A Skirt 2	_____	$15.00
Pitbulls In A Skirt 3	_____	$15.00
Pitbulls In A Skirt 4	_____	$15.00
Pitbulls In A Skirt 5	_____	$15.00
Victoria's Secret	_____	$15.00
Poison 1	_____	$15.00
Poison 2	_____	$15.00
Hell Razor Honeys	_____	$15.00
Hell Razor Honeys 2	_____	$15.00
A Hustler's Son	_____	$15.00
A Hustler's Son 2	_____	$15.00
Black and Ugly	_____	$15.00
Black and Ugly As Ever	_____	$15.00
Ms Wayne & The Queens of DC **(LGBTQ+)**	_____	$15.00
Black And The Ugliest	_____	$15.00
Year Of The Crackmom	_____	$15.00
Deadheads	_____	$15.00
The Face That Launched A Thousand Bullets	_____	$15.00
The Unusual Suspects	_____	$15.00
Paid In Blood	_____	$15.00
Raunchy	_____	$15.00
Raunchy 2	_____	$15.00
Raunchy 3	_____	$15.00
Mad Maxxx (4th Book Raunchy Series)	_____	$15.00
Quita's Dayscare Center	_____	$15.00
Quita's Dayscare Center 2	_____	$15.00
Pretty Kings	_____	$15.00
Pretty Kings 2	_____	$15.00
Pretty Kings 3	_____	$15.00
Pretty Kings 4	_____	$15.00
Silence Of The Nine	_____	$15.00

BY T. STYLES

Silence Of The Nine 2 _____ $15.00
Silence Of The Nine 3 _____ $15.00
Prison Throne _____ $15.00
Drunk & Hot Girls _____ $15.00
Hersband Material **(LGBTQ+)** _____ $15.00
The End: How To Write A _____ $15.00
Bestselling Novel In 30 Days (Non-Fiction Guide)
Upscale Kittens _____ $15.00
Wake & Bake Boys _____ $15.00
Young & Dumb _____ $15.00
Young & Dumb 2: Vyce's Getback _____ $15.00
Tranny 911 **(LGBTQ+)** _____ $15.00
Tranny 911: Dixie's Rise **(LGBTQ+)** _____ $15.00
First Comes Love, Then Comes Murder _____ $15.00
Luxury Tax _____ $15.00
The Lying King _____ $15.00
Crazy Kind Of Love _____ $15.00
Goon _____ $15.00
And They Call Me God _____ $15.00
The Ungrateful Bastards _____ $15.00
Lipstick Dom **(LGBTQ+)** _____ $15.00
A School of Dolls **(LGBTQ+)** _____ $15.00
Hoetic Justice _____ $15.00
KALI: Raunchy Relived _____ $15.00
(5th Book in Raunchy Series)
Skeezers _____ $15.00
Skeezers 2 _____ $15.00
You Kissed Me, Now I Own You _____ $15.00
Nefarious _____ $15.00
Redbone 3: The Rise of The Fold _____ $15.00
The Fold (4th Redbone Book) _____ $15.00
Clown Niggas _____ $15.00
The One You Shouldn't Trust _____ $15.00
The WHORE The Wind
Blew My Way _____ $15.00
She Brings The Worst Kind _____ $15.00
The House That Crack Built _____ $15.00
The House That Crack Built 2 _____ $15.00
The House That Crack Built 3 _____ $15.00
The House That Crack Built 4 _____ $15.00
Level Up **(LGBTQ+)** _____ $15.00
Villains: It's Savage Season _____ $15.00
Gay For My Bae **(LGBTQ+)** _____ $15.00
War _____ $15.00
War 2: All Hell Breaks Loose _____ $15.00
War 3: The Land Of The Lou's _____ $15.00
War 4: Skull Island _____ $15.00
War 5: Karma _____ $15.00
War 6: Envy _____ $15.00
War 7: Pink Cotton _____ $15.00
Madjesty vs. Jayden (Novella) _____ $8.99
You Left Me No Choice _____ $15.00
Truce – A War Saga (War 8) _____ $15.00
Ask The Streets For Mercy _____ $15.00
Truce 2 (War 9) _____ $15.00
An Ace and Walid Very, Very Bad Christmas (War 10) _____ $15.00
Truce 3 – The Sins of The Fathers (War 11) _____ $15.00
Truce 4: The Finale (War 12) _____ $15.00
Treason _____ $20.00
Treason 2 _____ $20.00

Hersband Material 2 **(LGBTQ+)**	_____	$15.00
The Gods Of Everything Else (War 13)	_____	$15.00
The Gods Of Everything Else 2 (War 14)	_____	$15.00
Treason 3	_____	$15.99
An Ugly Girl's Diary	_____	$15.99
The Gods Of Everything Else 3 (War 15)	_____	$15.99
An Ugly Girl's Diary 2	_____	$19.99
King Dom **(LGBTQ+)**	_____	$19.99
The Gods Of Everything Else 4 (War 16)	_____	$19.99
Raunchy: The Monsters Who Raised Harmony	_____	$19.99
An Ugly Girl's Diary 3	_____	$19.99
From Men To Monsters (War 17)	_____	$19.99
Pretty Kings 5	_____	$19.99
From Men To Monsters 2 (War 18)	_____	$19.99
A Weird Peace	_____	$19.99
Lemon	_____	$19.99

(**Redbone 1** & **2** are **NOT** Cartel Publications novels and if **ordered** the cost is **FULL** price of $16.00 **each plus shipping**. **No Exceptions**.)

Please add **$8.00** for shipping and handling fees for up to **(2)** **BOOKS PER ORDER**. (INMATES INCLUDED) (See next page for details)

The Cartel Publications * P.O. BOX 486 OWINGS MILLS MD 21117

Name: _____

Address: _____

City/State: _____

Contact/Email: _____

Please allow 10-15 BUSINESS days Before shipping.

PLEASE NOTE DUE TO COVID-19 SOME ORDERS MAY TAKE UP TO 3 WEEKS OR LONGER BEFORE THEY SHIP

The Cartel Publications is NOT responsible for Prison Orders rejected!

NO RETURNS and NO REFUNDS
NO PERSONAL CHECKS ACCEPTED
STAMPS NO LONGER ACCEPTED

BY T. STYLES